Ryan Madej

The Marianas Trench

ORBIS TERTIUS PRESS

Published by Orbis Tertius Press

ISBN: 978-1-7771304-0-4

To my son, Adrian, with infinite love.

So the darkness shall be the light,

and the stillness the dancing.

- T.S. Eliot

Passage (In)

My time fades in the rain as the night passes through the space of my fingers. The days are unimportant and obscure by my estimations, but as my narrative unfolds, perhaps the days, weeks, months, and years that have passed will have come into focus. The lounge I sit in is a stone's throw from the city limits; a city or a town (I can't seem to remember which) whose name I can't pronounce, where the clamor of bells and whistles from ships blends in beautifully with the hypnotic storm outside. Sheet lightning illuminates the darkness, thunder rattles in my head. The sea swells and recedes nearby like the images and thoughts through my mind. It's been three days since I've slept. I look around myself and see no sad faces, only joy and contentment. Yet, I cannot dissolve into a euphoric state like those around me. If I concentrate hard enough nobody seems to move. Frozen. Paralysis numbs these people right before my eyes. Lights flicker in the semi-darkness. My thought is half-finished, leaving me one complete breath before everything starts moving again. There are spots of blood on my sleeves, but no one seems to notice...

trickling

down

down to my wrists

I see the blade before my mind's eye, gleaming—the death instrument. I also see myself standing over her naked body, hand touching her breast, tongue seeking tongue. Then, nothing. That is where the thought ends. The whole of my story starts with her, or perhaps it's better to say Them, the Twins of my passions. I light a cigarette and order another drink. The night is young and I have much more to say.

....

The meek shall inherit the Earth; the meek shall inherit nothing. I closed my Bible long ago and opened this notebook in order to prove it. (These walls have shut me in.) I strain my eyes by looking off into the corners of the lounge, where a couple are swapping spit, their shapes turn into strange melting formations—a pile of liquid flesh.

-Sir, are you doing all right?

Looking up while concealing my sleeves, the buxom waitress, face and all, has begun to slip away from her bones just as the couple did a moment ago. Weakly smiling, I try to respond, but instead I just wave her away with my hands and let my face fall into my palms.

-We'll be closing in half an hour.

I barely hear what she says. The thunder and piano tinkles from a Beethoven sonata pass into nothingness. Tap, tap, tap, CRASH...tap, tap, tap, go the keys...then, CRASH goes the foot of God above me. Finally, I lift my pen.

The sonata has brought out the moon in my mind. That, and a sultry pair of eyes with a soft, penetrating gaze. I know those eyes. The moon greeted me one evening in the fall, looking as though the sky was engulfed by its sheer size, while I was on my way to see Ophelia. Hands in my pockets, smoking a sweet cigar, calmed by the silence. I stopped at a bench to admire the deep seas and craters that were highly visible that night. As I sat with the cigar dangling from my lips, I could see Ophelia's face in the moondust; sad, lonely. It had been weeks since I felt her skin...

Her teeth biting the pillow Her hands tied with silken
ribbon Her blood on my fingers

In a dream only days before she was cowering in a darkened corridor weakened by some intangible force, and I was standing over her waiting patiently for the death cry, my tears falling at her feet. I cannot explain it, but I felt a terror unlike any terror before as she screamed. The moon was full and it seemed to bleed crimson. I felt invigorated and chilled in equal doses.

....

The lounge is now closed for the evening; I am standing in the tiny foyer waiting for the rain to stop. Slipping my journal into my coat, I pull out my Zippo to light a cigarette. Not far away, the sea stretches out before me, and I see nothing but a deep blackness and I hear only the sound of the rain pounding the pavement. My hotel room awaits me, but I will not sleep. Stepping out into the downpour, the rain claws at me like a rabid animal attacking an unsuspecting stranger. I try to shield myself from its blows as I break into a run in the direction of the hotel. No lights guide me. Soon I'll be chilled to the bone.

....

The Hotel Room...

Where did I leave off ? Ophelia: too much water, so now I forbid my tears, but there is certainly more to say. I arrived at her apartment late that night. She answered the door wrapped in a silken kimono a friend had brought from Japan, her chestnut hair tied back and her lips a dark red.
"What took you so long, M.?" I told her I had stopped to admire the moon.

She laughed at my comment. Closing the door behind me I kissed her hard on the mouth. Cold, very cold lips, like kissing a corpse. One of her breasts, the left one—I remember because there was still the smallest evidence of a bite I had given her the last time—came tumbling out of the kimono, waiting for me to grasp it with my hands. Her hair glittered in the hallway light as I kneaded her breast, her peppermint breath warming my neck.

"First we need a pick-me-up" I recall her saying. I knew what she was referring to. On the table in the living room was the Theban meerschaum pipe shaped in the likeness of a blooming rose, cradling a piece of opium. Sitting down she opened her kimono, reclined with the pipe in hand, and beckoned me with her painted fingers.

Soon the room filled with smoke. The meerschaum turned a dark orange as we nearly lost sight of one another, but we were energetic enough to paw and intertwine our bodies; her lips were no longer cold. Somehow we found our way to her bedroom, whose lights had turned blue. Naked and drugged as we were—her skin the hue of a forgotten sea—I looped a piece of nylon rope around her neck and entered her from behind. My mind hurtled away from me as the rope tightened and our bodies moved in rhythm. As the night wore on, the opium wore off, and we sat upright in Ophelia's bed, lighting each other's cigarettes when she turned to me with her glazed eyes and suddenly became serious.

"Can I tell you something, M.? Something important? Or are you still too stoned to really talk about anything?"

Tapping out my smoke I turned onto my belly and asked her to continue.

"I've been wanting to cut again, M. Other than seeing you, I've really felt like I have nothing left to give the world but my body. In saying that, you have become the world to me, as fucking stupid as that sounds. Very little gives me any pleasure, only you."

"Should I be concerned?" I asked calmly.

"Maybe you should."

I laughed and proceeded to light another cigarette for her. She casually put it to her lips and shot me a look of disdain, probably because I hadn't given her the response she wanted. Opening the bedside drawer she produced a tiny blade, no bigger than a penknife, that held flecks of old blood. Leaning back on the pillow she played with the knife while she smoked...

"Do you believe in prophecy, M.?"

"Only in personal prophecy."

"So you're a prophet, then?"

"Something like that. Only, I dream of something more than being a prophet."

"And what would that be?" she asked curiously.

"That's for me to know and you to find out, my dear."

With those words she no longer questioned me, but I could tell I had left her intrigued.

As she put the blade away and flicked off the light, I turned on my side to look out the window, searching for the lunar disk. Nothing. With sleep slowly weighing upon me I remembered a prayer that had often given me solace. It went as follows: 'O Divine One, grant me the strength to pull the trigger. Grant me the wisdom to know when I have been more than a Sadist and a mediocre Masochist. Grant me these and I will worship you a thousand fold before it's all said and done. Amen.'

Closing my eyes, I felt myself smiling.

....

I'm alive. Despite my idea that I'm truly dead, a twitching in my mind keeps pounding out a signal that a remnant deep within me glows with a pale light. I'm back at the lounge, for the hotel was too silent and cold for my liking today. I stare blankly out of the window, my face half reflected in the glass. Pools of water have risen in the sunken concrete. I sit alone near the exit. The bartender is playing solitaire, a small cigar hanging from his lips, and his ashen features are clouded in smoke, disappearing and reappearing in waves. Waves like the sea, waves outside the window, waves of thought, cresting and foaming at the edges of my mind, ebbing and flowing. A svelte young woman with crimson hair sits down at the bar. She reminds me of the Other Twin, the one who got away; the one I've been after ever since she disappeared.

Before Ophelia, there was Red. After Red, only a series of dead ends. I can still vividly picture the night we met. The sky lit up in cherry blossom and citrus orange, the streets of Midtown alive with the usual intoxicating cries, empty banter, and strangeness. She wore black gloves, perfectly fitted to her slender fingers. Her facial dimensions were simple, but sharpened around the eyes, bringing out their pale blue. I could never look deeply into Red's eyes, for often there seemed to be a dark stream crossing over her face. She smoked Egyptian cigarettes and played chess.

Yes, chess. I had nearly forgotten her obsession with the game and its nostalgic flavours, systems, and general miscellany. During our first conversation together, I discovered she was a rather experienced player, consequently leading me into a match with her less than a week later...

She lived in one of the better areas of Midtown, deep in the Western Quarter in a stylish house that seemed to suit her tastes. Upon entering I noticed that she kept a wide collection of Japanese Noh masks on her wall, along with numerous odds and ends that felt foreign.

"Care for a drink before we sit down?"

"A scotch if you have it. Neat."

"Good choice. I'll join you in one of those."

As she prepared the drinks, I noticed the board had already been set up in the living room with the pieces perfectly aligned. We sat across from one another and clinked our glasses. I took the opportunity to light her cigarette, which she graciously accepted.

"You're very much the gentleman, which seems to be a rarity here in Midtown. Actually, when we ran into one another I had arrived by train that night. You offered me a light then, too. Are you always in the habit of picking up strange women?"

"If the mood strikes me."

"Well I'm glad it did. I could tell right away we would get along just fine."

"How so? Are you truly that insightful during first meetings?"

"My perceptions of people are rarely inaccurate, which comes from many years spent hunched over chess boards such as this one. I bought it in Prague several years ago when I was traveling through Europe."

"It really is beautiful."

"Yes. Shall we begin?"

The game progressed quickly, as did our consumption of scotch and cigarettes. By move twenty, I started to lose focus and I could see a different side of Red emerge on those sixty-four squares.

"Look at the board carefully before making a move."

"I prefer to move the pieces my own way, thanks."

"So in other words, stupidly and haphazardly? Is that what you're saying?"

Her hand hovered over a knight, blue smoke escaping from between her lips in tiny wisps. She moved it and managed to fork my queen and rook—the game, along with my sobriety, was slipping away from me.

"Say what you will about my play on the board, but I'm enjoying this."

"I suppose I was right about you," she said softly.

"How do you mean?"

"You rely more on instinct than logic, which is apparent from your play on the board. You can't see that far ahead, which is unfortunate. If you were able to, perhaps this game would have gone on a lot longer."

"Are you always such a bitch?"

She smiled.

"Only when the mood strikes me."

....

Evening again. The warm air of late summer drifts over my head as I look out to sea. The path between here, the hotel, and the lounge is all I've cared to traverse as I've drifted between the pages. It will be sunset soon and I should get inside to avoid the shadows, but I need some fresh air to continue...

In many ways, I was playing a winning game with Ophelia, for she often fell into my arms after being alone for so long. During the hours we continued to spend together, I began to feel a deep warmth grow within me. I began to see again, for I had been blind to my own power. Ophelia was truly mine for the taking, if I so chose. I came to realize this one night when we were stepping out for the evening at a private club in Midtown's Dragon Court.

"How did you get access to this place, M.? Special connections?"

"You could say that. I've spent as much time around the riff-raff of the Dragon Court as I've spent in libraries. I appreciate the dichotomy, and I've learned much from both."

"Such as?"

"Leave no stone unturned."

She stood close to me as we walked, practically enveloping herself in my trench coat. I lit a cigarillo and exhaled the smoke into the night. Ophelia had consumed too much wine before we departed and perhaps that was why she was clinging to me so tightly. As we stepped into the penumbra of a streetlight I could see her mascara running.

"Are you crying, Ophelia? My God, what's wrong with you tonight?"

"You won't leave my side tonight will you, M.? Promise that you'll stay close."

"I promise, though I have to tell you that where we're going is not for the squeamish."

Looking at me with large eyes and a weak smile, she returned to the crook of my arm without saying another word. My mind reeled at the thought of what the night was going to bring with Ophelia at my side. As we walked deeper into the Dragon Court and the light around us dispersed, I began to feel completely at ease, as though I were slipping under a warm blanket...

Future Proof

The Archive called late on a Saturday and asked me to come in as soon as possible. I grabbed my coat and hopped the next train from the Outskirts into Midtown, practically running through the corridors of the Hall of Records and Old Library to my familiar desk with its mountain of files. One file in particular—the one everyone would be envious to have—sat neatly at the foot of the mountain, wrapped nicely in dark blue paper.

-It was dropped off this afternoon.

The Director was standing at my desk, clutching a series of files, a grave look on his face.

-Process this quickly and archive it. No need to dwell too long on the contents. He must be dead by now, as this package seems to indicate.

-How do you figure? He hasn't been in Midtown in years. Maybe this is just what he intended.

The Director sat down on my desk and looked at me very intently, quietly lighting a cigarette without averting his gaze.

-Remember, our duty here is to preserve materials, not exploit them. I want this processed within the next two weeks and the report finalized. Understood?

-Yes, sir...no problem.

Rising, he crushed the cigarette in my overflowing ashtray and walked off to his office. I heard every step as we were the only two people there. Gently unwrapping the package I began to see just how much material awaited me. The manuscript was neatly handwritten on high grade paper and seemed to emit a scent of the sea, salty and warm. Leaning back in the chair I picked up a handful of pages and began to read.

The Marianas Trench
by Mantra Hand

"The continuous work of our life is to build death."
- Michel de Montaigne

That first sentence, though it was not his own, put its tentacles around me and began to squeeze, gently at first...

....

When I came into possession of the journals, letters, and collages collected under *The Marianas Trench* by Mantra Hand, I felt as though the quantum field had grown and placed a large piece of gold in my hands. Everyone in Midtown had heard the name before, but only a handful had ever seen the face or spoken to the man who had written several masterful works over the course of only a few years, one of which, *The Black Roses*, still sits on my shelf. For those who knew about him through his writings and strange interviews, it was assumed that he was writing a final masterpiece, but after his disappearance no one expected this, least of all myself. That was until the manuscript arrived at the Archive. When something comes into the Archive it means one of two things: either the person is deceased, or the person has consciously chosen to have the material archived. Neither one of these conditions could be confirmed by any source...Midtown has only one way in and out, and Mantra Hand left the party early.

....

The rules of the Archive do not allow those who work there to take material home, so that night I read as much as possible before fatigue set in, highlighting key points with asterisks and annotations as I progressed, though this didn't stop me from photocopying a few pages here and there for my own delight, being a fan and all. Processing the book and never seeing it again did not appeal to me. The first section titled *The Door*, though brief and cryptic—which most of his work was, with the exception of *The Black Roses*—had all the usual Mantra Hand trappings.

(The Door)

The Door always swings inward, for that is what I've been told in the distant past by those people who have crossed over the Threshold. Those same people never returned. Their voices come to me through invisible means known as the Muted Horn*. The entrance to the Door is always *changing*. Keep that in mind if you're ever trying to find me. This is as much a guide as it is a story, so listen carefully. All that preceded these pages was a preamble to a disappearance alluded to at an earlier time that hopefully fell into the hands of my biographer*. I'll begin by giving you a survey of my thoughts at the present time. My location is unknown, even to me, but I dare say that I'll be liberated. I should probably begin with a *dramatis personae* of sorts, small and precise.

The Muted Horn is unreliable, but I'm not going to get into the aspects of its nature. That, my friends, is a difficult task that even I'm not up to these days. In saying that, the Muted Horn may have been responsible for my current predicament, not to mention the appearance of R. in my life. R. is the epitome of the grand gesture, the terra incognita, and the femme fatale. A combination that is both rare and deadly, though not in the physical sense. I had hoped—perhaps naively and obsessively—that opening the Door would lead me to her again, but as I began to search her out, I questioned why I would want to find someone who had caused me so much chaos in so little time. The point cannot be stressed enough that Midtown is a place that forever remains *foreign* to me, even after decades within its walls. R. was very much the same way—elusive, of unknown origin, destined to remain a mystery even after a lifetime in her presence. My time with her was limited—though often it felt like a thousand lifetimes—yet despite that fact, like the Door, much more opened up for me...for better or worse.

....

...After the initial reading I walked to a nearby hotel for a nightcap, looking over my shoulder hoping the Director didn't send someone after me. He did that sort of thing to people he didn't trust with sensitive information. Just by looking at me, the Director could tell I might try to pull the wool over his eyes, yet he had no choice but to give me the package because he knew I had a deep interest in Mantra Hand. My face and hands tingled as I walked the nearly invisible footpath that snaked its way through the smaller inconspicuous areas of the city—places virtually vacant, shadowy, and lifeless during the day—before abruptly ending mere blocks from the Dragon Court in the foreign district.

Only half a dozen lights illuminated the path between Salamander Road and the divide at the Marble Corridor where I heard a voice call out from beneath one of the lamps. His face, half in the obsidian blackness, the other half looking at me with a dull gaze, beckoned me gruffly to step into the light.

-Do you have a cigarette, friend? I'm fresh out.

-Yeah sure. Is that all you want?

His eyes glazed over. The glow from the moon seemed to turn what I could see of his profile a deathly blue.

-All I want is a cigarette, yes.

Opening a fresh pack, I handed him one, flicking the

lighter alive.

-Don't need a light. Have my own thanks.

Slipping a cigarette between my lips, I let the naked flame send me the nicotine bliss. I stood there for a moment before walking off.

-Thanks my friend. Hopefully we will run into each other again.

Turning around I could no longer make out any trace of him. All that remained was the smoking butt of the cigarette, burning out in a badly tended flowerbed. I threw my photocopies in the nearest garbage can and walked a little faster.

....

A little known fact: If you sleep in a cold room, you are more likely to have a bad dream. My room at the Hotel Papillion that night felt like an icebox as I staggered in around 3 in the morning. Six double gin and tonics. Two words kept echoing in my head so I wouldn't forget the next day when I awoke: Muted Horn. They were repeated in my slurred mind speech as I sat by the window and looked across the empty plaza. Barren trees. "Winter is coming," I thought to myself, "pale, cold, and dead." I fell asleep in the chair with my clothes on and dreamed of being buried alive in a snowstorm.

....

-You look like death warmed over. What happened to you?

Sandra. I looked up from the pile of papers in front of me and saw her standing there, her black hair shiny and immaculate. She worked on the other half of the floor but we often ran into one another in the stacks. That day she was wearing a blue cashmere sweater and tight black skirt. To say I wanted to sleep with her was an understatement, but we were stuck in first gear, mainly due to my lack of charm. I stared at her blankly for a moment before responding.

-I've been nursing a hangover. I need to get back to my apartment and shower, shave. What are you doing here on a Sunday, anyway?

-I could ask you the very same thing, but I know the answer. You hit the jackpot, didn't you?

Even in a place like the Archive with its quiet

sensibilities news travels fast. Too fast. I turned away and lit a cigarette (my fourth) and finished my coffee (my third), trying my best not to look at her directly for two reasons: she looked stunning, and I didn't really want to get into too much detail regarding the manuscript.

-So are you going to remain coy, or are we going to have a little chat about your score later? she whispered.

-Maybe. Come back around three. I'll be ducking out around then and heading back to the Outskirts.

-I'll see you then.

I didn't dare look at her as she walked away thinking she might notice, so I looked out the window instead and saw that it had started to rain. "Fuck," I thought, "I didn't bring an umbrella." Sandra probably brought one with her that day. She was the type who was always prepared. Fate smiled on me that day, and a little bit of radiance broke through the murky gloom.

....

Three o'clock came around faster than I had anticipated, and my thoughts were still sunk deeply into the meaning of the Muted Horn. Sandra appeared at my desk with a wry smile and her umbrella. Closing my laptop, I put on my overcoat and we slowly made our way through the halls, our footsteps echoing deeply. Sandra was still smiling.

-Did you make any progress this afternoon? she asked.

-Not much.

-Mmm. Sounds like the fan boy is having some trouble, eh?

I said nothing.

-I suppose you don't know that I wrote several papers on Mantra Hand back in college. He has been something of an obsession of mine for a long time. I mean, why wouldn't he be? He's the best writer Midtown has produced. I envy you.

-I wrote a paper on him too.

-Oh?

-A few years ago. I published it in a small literary journal. It was called *The Transmutation of Mantra Hand.*

-Interesting title. We should compare notes sometime. I

live in the Western Quarter if you ever want to drop by for coffee.

-Are you asking me out?

-Maybe. It's something you should have done a while back. We could have had some great talks about Mantra by now. Here's my number. Use it.

She opened her umbrella and stepped out into the mist, not even saying goodbye or turning to wave. I needed a smoke and realized I was fresh out. The long train ride out of the city was going to feel a lot longer today now that I was having a nic fit. Rubbing my face and turning up my collar, I ran to the station. I was the only passenger that afternoon and I quickly fell asleep by the window. When I arrived back in the Outskirts the rain had stopped, but it had created a landscape awash in deep tones of a forest mushroom blue. My apartment was freezing and far too silent. Unopened mail, unwatched movies, and untouchable Chinese food sat on my coffee table. I wondered if Sandra had made it home. An hour went by, then two. I couldn't sit still so I picked up the phone, dialing the number as fast as I could. No answer, only the machine.

-Hey Sandra. Would you want to meet up tonight if possible? I can take the train back into the city in a couple hours. Call me if you get this.

Walking over to the bookshelf, I pulled down my copy of Mantra's *The Black Roses* and flipped to a page I had marked, noticing a highlighted passage...

"On a clear night in the Northern hemisphere, the naked eye can discern approximately five thousand stars—all of them beautiful, and all of them dead long ago. If Earth were a star we would appear the same way to some alien world. Beautiful, but equally dead."

As I finished reading, the phone rang. Sandra. Picking up the receiver I barely had the chance to say hello.

-My address is 1120 Salamander Road. I'll be waiting outside. See you soon.

Click. Dial tone. Half an hour later I was out the door with the copy of *The Black Roses* stuffed into my overcoat, peering at the monolithic buildings that were slowly becoming shrouded in the evening fog as the train made its way toward the Marble Corridor. I flipped through the pages of the book to see if I had highlighted any additional passages, perhaps hoping I would be given a clue in connection to my current task. Nothing, not even a scribble in the margins. Closing the book, I began to think about Sandra and just how quickly things had come together in such a wonderful, yet odd way. It felt like a well constructed dream, and if it was, I didn't want to wake up from it anytime soon. Salamander Road was unusually quiet that night, even for a Sunday, as I casually made my way through the Western Quarter toward Sandra's home. The further I walked from the core the darker it seemed to get, as though the clouds had descended onto the streets. Thankfully, Sandra was one of the few to have the sense to keep a light on. Most of the other houses looked like silhouettes drowning in the burgeoning fog. She sat on her front step bundled in a black pea coat, sipping coffee when she noticed me approaching.

-You made it, I see. I guess we have a lot of time to make up for, don't we?

Zeitgeist

The world has decided to go on for one more day. I have gone on as well, but in no particular direction other than inward. Today is Monday; it feels like a Monday. From what I hear on a distant radio there is a thirty percent chance it will rain again. I look out the window at the barely perceptible sea and realize how calm it is. Another cigarette, another sip of wine, and an abundance of paper, so I write. Where I am was never important; it's where I'm going. Somewhere bells are tolling. The fans above me twirl endlessly, much like the ground beneath our feet, going round and round to nowhere. My throat is dry.

Where to begin again? Really I should begin where I left off with Ophelia as we drifted into the club deep in the Dragon Court. Her rigid frame clinging to mine as we walked down the dimly lit flight of stairs into the lobby. A fair-haired woman in a PVC outfit greeted us at the door. We had met before...

"Mr. H.? It has been a long time since you made a visit. Oh, and I see you have brought someone with you this time."

"Say hello, Ophelia, don't be shy," I said tapping her cheek with my palm.

Ophelia eked out a grim smile.

"It's her first time here, so we should probably go a little easy on her. Would you please find me a suitable girl?"

The woman gave me a gracious little bow and told us to relax in the lounge while we waited for a room to become available.

"Come on now Ophelia, we're going to sit down and have a little chat."

"Just don't leave my side, M."

"Don't you worry...I'll be here the whole time."

Ophelia and I. That sounds remarkably strange without her flesh before me, teasing me with her hollow words and actions, breathing all that emptiness into my waiting mouth. Ophelia the drowned one, the daughter of lost memory, the limp flower.

We sat on a large crushed velvet couch and ordered a couple drinks while we waited. She looked at me with apprehension, perhaps because I could not erase the deep grin on my face.

"What is this place, M.? You never cared to tell me the name."

"That will remain a little secret."

"Why can't you tell me? I deserve to know."

"One thing I would like to make clear is that not everyone deserves to know everything, my dear, only a privileged few. And even those people probably should not see the truth."

"The truth of what? You're starting to piss me off with these cryptic answers of yours."

My smile disappeared. She understood and retreated with her anger.

"The truth of what is to become of this city of ours. But in answer to your question about our location, I'll tell you this: it's not a place for the weak. I've brought you here because, well, I'm not always kind."

She tried to get up to leave, but I grabbed her arm and cradled her.

"Now, now, Ophelia, let's not become restless and afraid. I told you I wouldn't leave your side. Drink up."

The silence between us grew heavy as we waited...eventually Ophelia found the courage to speak again, this time in softer tones.

"You're not who I thought you were M. and that scares me."

"I've come to that conclusion myself after many years too, Ophelia. Do you know I write books?"

"No, though I'm not surprised."

"Well, I've written a few works, all of which have been critically acclaimed and sold relatively well. This allows me to enjoy the lifestyle that I do, which has become decadent, making me weak. Remember what I just said about weakness? Anyway, losing the creative drive can only lead a person, at least in my mind, in the other direction."

"And what direction is that?"

"You know the answer Ophelia, you have been walking in that direction for a long time. Come on now, be a sport and humor me for once."

I could tell I hit the softest part of her with my words, and that she knew what I was implying.

"Death. You're speaking of death."

"Yes, Ophelia, death."

A door at the far end of the room opened and my fair haired beauty came to our table, bubbly as ever, dangling a key in her hand.

"Your room is ready. Silvi will be your woman for the evening. Enjoy."

Ophelia grasped my arm hard, digging her nails into my flesh, a series of fresh tears welling at the edges of her eyes.

"It's time to go now, Ophelia. If you truly want me then follow my lead like a good girl."

Of course she followed, as I knew she would. What choice did she really have in that situation? We entered the room. A large bed took up the majority of the space, and upon the bed was the woman named Silvi—raven haired, buxom, naked.

"Good evening. You must be Mr. H. Who is this with you?" she asked.

"This is Ophelia."

"What a beautiful name. Tragic, but beautiful."

We both laughed. I could feel Ophelia's nails dig even

deeper into me and her heart beginning to race as I told her to strip down to her underwear.

"Silvi would you be so kind as to take care of the rest?"

"With pleasure, sir."

Silvi flashed a subtle smile as she began unclasping Ophelia's bra, and Ophelia mildly resisted, still partially grasping me as her panties were lowered to the floor with Silvi's immaculate teeth.

"You've done this before, haven't you?" Silvi asked.

Ophelia opened her mouth but remained silent.

"Ophelia, the nice lady asked you a question," I said quietly, palming a handful of her hair and jerking her head back, giving Silvi the opportunity to plant a kiss on her neck.

"Yes," she moaned, "a long time ago with a friend."

"Good. I knew you had a voice."

They moved to the bed while I undressed and got comfortable in a chair, anxious to watch the opening of the game before entering it myself. Ophelia's eyes were closed, and her body appeared rigid as Silvi mounted her—yet her mouth was agape, and a trellis of hair dangled between her fingers as the snake-like tongue of Silvi licked the void between her legs. From my coat I produced the tiny blade of Ophelia's, which I had stolen from her bedside drawer.

"Ophelia my dear, give me your arm."

She could barely address me as Silvi had worked her close to orgasm. The smell of sweat and fluids permeated the room as I clutched her thin arm in my hand and cut. The blood flowed and I could no longer tell if Ophelia's screams were of pain or joy. It didn't matter to me anyway; I had given her a moment to decide what meant more to her: pleasure or pain. Silvi raised her head and licked the blood from my fingers without a word. Ophelia opened her eyes and saw me standing over her, a look of confusion, shock, and bliss across her face.

"M., you're a bastard."

"You may be right, Ophelia. You may be right."

I thanked Silvi for her assistance and tongued her beautiful mouth before getting dressed.

Ophelia pawed at her wound, trying her best to staunch the flow of blood.

"I must be on my way now, Ophelia. Call me if you get the chance."

"Fuck you, M. Fucking go to hell."

Turning around I smiled and waved, leaving in the softest way possible by shutting the door gently and I walked back into the Midtown night feeling at ease. As my feet took me through the Northern section of the Dragon Court, the mescaline and weed dealers occupied their corners as usual, their eyes peeled for the nighttime ramblers who needed a quick fix. Angel dust, black hollies, meth, a whole glorious rainbow of altered consciousness waiting to be sold. A group of whores inhaled heroin near the Blue Room, desperately trying to seduce the drunken men who staggered outside. Vacant eyes, ruby lips...One day they will all burn, I thought. Walking past them they lowered their eyes, actually backing away as though a mere gaze in my direction would kill them.

"An unholy glow," one of them whispered. "An unholy glow."

....

My pen stops moving. I stare at the remainder of the wine in my glass and swirl it around thinking of Ophelia's blood on my fingertips that night: warm, like a river under a hot sun. I've come to know many rivers since my departure from Midtown, small and large, but none so inspiring as the Ganges during the *Avatarana*, the time in which throngs of bathers gather in the waters in order to purge themselves of ten sins. Even in the fading light I could see people wading up to their necks, deep in prayer, asking the heavens for forgiveness. As night fell I continued to stare at the slow movements of the water, sending the sins away. I remember laughing at the prospect of bathing in such a sacred place, knowing only ten sins could be erased. Two handfuls, that was all.

The sea is still calm, and I can see from my window that the lounge lights have begun to dim as the deep blue night approaches over the horizon. On evenings like these I would go for walks through Midtown's Western Quarter, usually finding my way to Red's house that was surrounded by beautiful birch trees and well-tended hedges. The night I left Ophelia I walked until I arrived on Red's doorstep, hoping she would answer. I knocked.

The door slowly opened and she looked at me strangely...

"It's you. What are you doing here? I wasn't expecting you."

"I was out for a walk and decided to drop in."

"I can see that. What do you want?"

"I wanted to see you. Can I come in for a while?"

She thought about it for a moment before opening the door. Her living room was pitch black, so I gathered she was getting ready for bed. She wore a violet nightgown with tiny flowers, an ample amount of cleavage showing off her milky white skin. That was the first time I glimpsed her in such a revealing way.

"Something to drink, M.? A nightcap?"

"Whatever you're having."

She set down two scotches and lit a cigarette, a look of feigned hospitality on her face. A book lay open on her coffee table—The Occult Origins of Midtown—a little known masterpiece. Red noticed my interest and promptly picked it up.

"Have you read this before, M? That's a first edition signed by the author. He's an old friend."

"Yes, I've read it several times, very intriguing. You know William Pawel?"

"We used to fuck every now and then when I first came to Midtown."

"Is that so? I had the impression you had better taste. He's not a very attractive man, from what I've seen. Brilliant academic. That book is incredible."

"Intelligence is not a prerequisite for sex with me, nor is a wonderful body. He had what I was looking for, then I was done with him. Why I'm telling you this I don't know."

She downed her scotch and quickly lit another cigarette. Feeling a little brave I got up and began perusing the bookshelves.

"Did you just come by tonight to finger my books or did you have something else in mind?"

"I really didn't have anything in particular in mind, but since I saw that book I've begun to think I'm missing something about you."

"The feeling is mutual. Care for a quick game before you leave?"

"Did I say I was leaving?" I said with a snicker.

By this point she was next to me leaning against the bookshelf, blowing smoke in my face.

"If you're under the impression that we're going to fuck just because we've shared a night together over a game of chess, you're sadly mistaken. However, I will gladly play you again and talk shop before I send you on your way. Deal?"

She extended her hand in an almost mocking gesture. I accepted.

"A little more sure of yourself this time?" She smirked, her cigarette dangling from her lips.

"Not at all, but I'll stick around for the chance to converse and pick your brain a little."

"All right. Pick away."

She drew the blinds and brought over the bottle of scotch before setting up the board and turning on some music—The Room of Mirrors, Abandoned Cities, and The Algebra of Darkness—all Harold Budd pieces if I remember correctly. I began to slip out of my thoughts about Ophelia, feeling suddenly smaller and weaker in Red's presence. She cast a large shadow on the wall, setting the mood for our game.

I sipped my scotch and we began to play.

"Since you brought him up, how did you come to know William Pawel?"

"You don't waste any time with your questions, do you? We met at a small gathering of rare book dealers, a private gathering for people interested in Midtown's history. This wasn't long after I arrived here, and I had heard that he was quite the brilliant academic, just like you pointed out."

"Strange that we didn't meet each other in a situation such as that."

"How so?" she whispered while moving out her knight.

"I'm a writer, as you may have guessed."

"You? What have you written? Anything of note?"

"A few novels that have allowed me to live moderately well."

"Hmmm, William never mentioned any local talent."

"I've kept most aspects of my life fairly low key. William was one of the few people I did interviews with. Funny how he never mentioned any beautiful women in his life."

Red laughed, nearly choking on her scotch.

"I would like to point out that we had a very discreet relationship. To be perfectly honest with you, he was forbidden to speak about me to anyone."

"Oh? He was that subservient to you?"

"Yes he was...I also like to live low-key. Midtown has provided that for me in spades, at least for the moment."

"I kind of figured you to be something of a nomad. It's easy to see that you're well traveled. The masks on the wall give it away."

Red paused for a moment to look at them, a deep smile forming on her glistening lips.

"I've always been very partial to the last one in the series."

"The one with the two characters?"

"Yes."

"What do they mean?"

"Apocalypse."

The moment that she said that word I had to sit back and laugh—a cold, lifeless laugh—but a laugh just the same. A word that echoed throughout centuries fell upon her lips and it actually meant something. Maybe it was in that instance, so familiar and inviting, that I caught a glimpse of her that I wanted to pursue to the end, the very End...

"What do all the others mean then, if that's a sign of the Omega?" I asked casually.

She looked at me coldly, her smile instantly gone.

"You know that not everything gets revealed all at once, right? Sometimes never."

"Fine. You win."

"You're a fast learner...I always win."

"I suppose I have much to learn about you."

She leaned back and finished her scotch, dismissing me with a wave of her hand.

"This was not a good night for you to show up. All your questions have put me in a foul mood. You can see yourself out. Goodnight."

I finished my cigarette and watched her slip out of the room and into the depths of sleep. Turning off the stereo and light I gently made my way out, much like I had earlier in the evening with Ophelia. Walking back through the desolate Midtown streets I felt the presence of those two women hovering, matching my every step. My body felt heavy, dense. When I finally made it to bed I dreamed of the pair of them standing on either side of me, naked, as I looked at my tired reflection in the bathroom mirror. Their lips came together.

Now they only appear as ghosts...

Name Taken

-You didn't waste any time getting here. Care to go for a little walk around the Quarter?

-Sure, I don't often get out this far anymore.

-You like to stay on the fringes, don't you? Sandra smirked.

-Yeah, I suppose. The Outskirts are quieter for my kind of living these days.

-What kind of living is that?

-The solitary kind.

She handed me a coffee and we kept heading west

toward Bastion Perrot square, a place she described as great for conversation, as the Quarter had no tolerance for the kind of sleaze one saw in the other districts of Midtown. The air was moist and light and it made me feel a little more relaxed. She asked me for a smoke, which caught me off guard as I hadn't seen her light up before.

-A kind of personal indulgence, in much the same way Mantra Hand has become. Wouldn't you agree?

-Ah...sure...You know, Sandra, I really shouldn't be discussing this file with you.

-So then why did you come all the way out here? Just for shits and giggles?

-I'm not sure. Why did you invite me in the first place?

-Don't try to deflect. You came out here because you want to get in my pants, right? I've seen the way you look at me around the office. Personally I think it's kind of flattering, considering you're less than forward in your intentions. On top of that, you're in possession of something I want, and I'm not just talking about your cock. Do you see where I'm going with this?

-You want to know what I'm reading.

-My you're perceptive. I'm not being totally sarcastic either. I looked up your article on Mantra...Intelligent work. A little pedantic perhaps, but overall a fine piece. But yes, I want in on this badly.

-Well you certainly get to the point.

-Tell me I'm wrong and we'll call it a night.

-No, you're right...I need your help...Maybe in more ways than one.

She snuffed out her cigarette, and drew herself closer to me as we approached the square. A flock of pigeons fluttered about the statue of Bastion Perrot, Midtown's founder. His bronze eyes looked east down Salamander Road, named after a famous incident where Perrot allegedly walked through flames unscathed. Sandra looked at the statue and then at me.

-Do you know very much about Bastion Perrot? I've only heard a few snippets here and there.

-He was one of the key figures in the founding of Midtown, along with his wife Madeleine de Garza, his friend Hanz Overbeck, and a mysterious Japanese man who was simply known as Junichiro. The Western Quarter was Perrot's. The rest of Midtown was divided amongst the rest and designed by them. All were purported to dabble in the esoteric arts.

-You make similar claims about Mantra's involvement in esotericism in your essay. You don't think he's dead, do you?

-Not from what I've read so far.

-Which begs the question: are you ever going to tell me the juicy tidbits?

I paused, trying to think the situation through without succumbing to my desire for her. Difficult. I found it very difficult. She looked particularly ravishing in the twilight glow. What else could I do but submit?

-Have you ever heard of something called the Muted Horn, Sandra?

-Only in a fictional sense.

-How do you mean?

-That sounds just like the Trystero. You know, from *The Crying of Lot 49*. It was a phantom mailing system that was never proven to exist. Mantra makes mention of

51

this in the manuscript?

-Yes. He says voices come to him through the Horn, but at the same time he calls it unreliable, not fully grasping what it is exactly. There is also mention of a Door. Some sort of metaphor I would assume.

-Can we really come to assume anything with Mantra Hand? I mean, he doesn't even use his real name. Have you ever really thought about his name and what that might mean?

-Like a lot of other readers I've found it to be a bit on the strange side, but a lot of writers are strange, right?

Sandra shook her head and took a long sip of coffee before continuing. She asked me for another cigarette, which I lit for her, catching a whiff of cinnamon as she inhaled.

-His name obviously says something about his character. Think about it: a mantra is a sacred syllable or groups of words capable of bringing about transformative actions. The hand is used to write or create. So in essence he is conjuring something spiritual. How was that not obvious to you?

-Maybe I'm just not as insightful as you.

-You might be right. Did he mention anything else?

-A biographer. Who the hell that could be is anyone's guess. I find it a little difficult to believe he would divulge aspects of his life to just anybody...I mean, would you Sandra, if you had a literary reputation like his?

-Probably not.

We were silent for what seemed like a very long time; we didn't even move. Only the light blue smoke from our cigarettes floated between us. The moon was full and the stars hung luminously in the sky. I fondled the book in my coat pocket and I thought about the passage in The Black Roses I had read. I felt sick to my stomach, as though Mantra Hand were as far away as those stars. Sandra broke the silence.

-Do you want to head back to my place?

-Maybe I should just catch the next train back to the Outskirts, it's getting late...I need to be in the office early to work on the archiving of the manuscript.

She looked me square in the face and flashed a wicked

smile.

-You're not going to chicken out now, are you? You know I wasn't joking about what I said, right?

-It's hard to tell with you, Sandra. When you think about it we really don't know each other that well.

-And that's going to stop you?

-I didn't say that...

....

Shafts of sunlight sliced through the blinds in Sandra's bedroom. I couldn't tell what time it was, as my watch was nowhere to be found. She was asleep, the curve of her breasts heaving at the top of the sheets, and a handful of her hair spread across the pillow. The night was a blur of tangled limbs, sucking, and moans that managed to leave a bad taste in my mouth...Not that sleeping with Sandra was terrible by any means, but I feared what came next. I found my watch next to a used condom and quickly got dressed, slipping out of her house and into the cool morning. I was already an hour late. As much as I wanted to rush in that morning, I took my time to sort out my thoughts. Patting my pockets, I realized I was out of cigarettes again. All I could taste was lead. Flashes of Sandra's body flickered through my mind in rapid succession and I suddenly felt ill. I vomited in a trashcan before regaining my bearings. Luckily the streets were virtually empty at that time of day so no one could see my gross act. The Archive, which I could see in the distance, only made me feel worse. The ride up in the elevator gave a slight reprieve to my sickness, but as I made my way into the office the Director was sitting at my desk with his feet up, pawing through the manuscript, his dark spectacles on the tip of his nose.

-I see that you finally made it in. A wee bit late, hmm?

-Yes, it would appear so.

A vague, smarmy smile appeared on his face, his fingers tapping the pages.

-You haven't made much progress on this. Shall I give this project to someone more capable?

-No, no...I'm sorry. My mind has been a little preoccupied but I assure you, sir, the work will be done on time.

-Feeling a bit stressed? You do look more pale than usual. Maybe I should have Sandra work with you on this. The two of you chat every now and then, right? By the way, did you happen to see her on your way in?

My heart stopped.

-No, sir. I haven't seen her since we left the office on the weekend.

-Care for a smoke? Looks like you could use a pick-me-up.

-Umm, sure. Thank you, sir...I'm fresh out.

He got up slowly, leaving the cigarette on top of the barely edited pages.

-Oh, and if you see Sandra please tell her to come see me right away.

-I'll be sure to do that.

I sat down and quickly lit the cigarette, glancing over my shoulder to make sure he was gone before picking up the manuscript. The office was deathly quiet, as though everyone had decided not come back once the weekend was over. Smart move. I should have done the same. My hands trembled a little as I picked up the pages again and began to read, pen in hand, fearing the manuscript would somehow swallow me whole...

(The Threshold)

The path beyond the Door is only sparsely lit, so traversing the terrain becomes an exercise in keeping oneself sane. Like Theseus following Ariadne's thread in the labyrinth of the Minotaur, there are many byways, dead ends, false walls, and Others one may encounter along the way. Yes, in addition to R. there were Others who played a part in the grand unified theory that I'm proposing on these pages. Of course, my belief is that there were a series of invisible players* as well, who may or may not have had a hand in my exile into darkness. Maybe I'm just slightly paranoid...Or maybe I fear I'll be found out in the End. Ha ha. Perhaps I shouldn't be so anxious to give myself away. Though truth be told, I've really said nothing. My destiny was, and will continue to be, defined by action. R. knew this, too. She was not a humble, withdrawn woman; as a matter of fact she was quite the opposite, having a vast knowledge in arts such as herbal medicine, hand-to-hand combat, and various other techniques picked up along the way.

....

Muted Horn, Biographer, Invisible Players, Door, Threshold... Who was this R.?, I asked myself...What did he mean by his destiny being defined by *action*? The words seemed to jumble together in my head along with a shaded black and white still of Sandra, who seemed to know so much more than I did about my subject. I felt faint. Closing my eyes, I tried to imagine the shape of the labyrinth he mentioned but came up with *nothing*. He said it himself in the passage: "Though truth be told, I've really said *nothing*." I notated all this in the summary, fatigued, even though I had barely begun. I read on...

(The Path)

"It is the city of mirrors, the city of mirages, at once solid and liquid, at once air and stone." - Erica Jong

An apt description of life within these walls. Midtown owes as much to an ancient city like Damascus as it does to more modern metropolises like New York or Prague; they exist as dark mazes on a horizon that is quickly getting darker. Again I should laugh because I get too far ahead of myself, spouting off when I should be focusing on the task at hand. I have not fully traversed this zone of desire, but inevitably it led me closer to R. without actually seeing her. She was an avid chess player, which I found unusual because she didn't appear to have the temperament for complicated systems and variations. She also had a flair for the esoteric, often engaging in conversations about long dead mystics and the like, trying to glean something from their knowledge. Perhaps that is why she came to Midtown in the first place, as it is known for its long history of strange and wild stories often involving Bastion Perrot, the founder of Midtown. Coming from the Outskirts like I did, one could only imagine Midtown as being founded by people of unusual and odd personalities...

It was as though Mantra walked beside me, or at least in my thoughts. I pictured Sandra and myself sitting in front of Perrot's statue the night before, trying to cobble together some sort of theory. Picking up the phone, I tried calling Sandra. She didn't answer. I needed more nicotine and caffeine in my system so I headed down the empty halls and through the Annex into the underground shops that were quickly falling into disuse. Lights flickered and half of the shops were barred by metal shutters. A deep echo resonated as I walked. Midtown was becoming a city of ghosts; a city of the dead. Mantra was from the Outskirts just like me, daring to enter the walls of Midtown only to find himself in a fading wasteland. Thinking about his cryptic sentences made me feel weak. I tried calling Sandra again, only this time from my cell. She picked up on the second ring, a quiet tone to her voice.

-Hello Sandra, it's me.

-Are you at the Archive? Did the Director ask about me?

-Yeah. He asked if I saw you come in this morning. He was looking through the manuscript and suggested that you take over my work.

-I'm flattered.

-Maybe you should do it. I'm not sure I'm up to the task.

-Come on now, are you *really* going to give me the prize this early in the game? Did sleeping with me last night soften you up?

-About that...

-Listen, what happened was nice and between two consenting adults. Leave it at that.

-All right...Are you coming in today?

-Probably not. Meet me tonight at the Waterfront Market. We'll talk then. 7pm.

-Do I have a choice?

-Of course you do, but you'll come. I mean, what else are you going to do?

....

The Director left earlier than usual that day, glancing at me before making his way out. He hadn't bothered to check on my progress which I found both unusual and satisfying as he had seemed fairly unapproachable since the manuscript slid across my desk. The work became more daunting, but as I continued to read Mantra Hand felt closer, despite the fact that what he had written seemed composed in code.

(The Wall)

Once you walk a little further, you will inevitably hit a Wall; a Wall that is so high that you will be unable to reach the top. With that in mind you may need to detour or find a way over the wall itself, though I must say that is not an easy task. One may have to access the Muted Horn, though one must know where it is in the first place. That can also prove to be difficult, as only the privileged with 24/7 access tend to know where it is at any given time. R. was one of those people of privilege. I once asked her, after we had finished watching Woman in the Dunes*, if I could ever see the Muted Horn up close. She laughed her usual robust laugh and told me that the Horn went by many other names and in reality I had probably encountered it without realizing it was there in the first place. I asked her to teach me more. Another round of laughter pealed off into the night air and faded quickly. She was already too far gone on an unknown mission that involved only her, like a solitary walk toward the gates of death. She seemed unafraid of wherever she was going, for she knew exactly how she was going to get there relatively unscathed. And then I followed with my own set of keys...So much for saying nothing about the Muted Horn.

I made sure to notate *Woman in the Dunes*, a film I had never watched, adding it to my running list of unknowns about the manuscript. Looking out the window, I could see that the light was slowly slipping away over the horizon. My meeting with Sandra loomed. There was no point in asking myself what came next, for in some way I knew that the further I went down the spiral the more obscured and confusing my situation would become...Like Sandra said: what else was I going to do? Lighting a cigarette and putting on my coat, I made my way into the spectral Midtown evening alone and on foot. Scores of people flooded the streets, lost in their own worlds: staring at the pavement or hiding their faces behind the collars of overcoats, crouching in doorways reading books, feeding crows and pigeons, even the odd person crying into a cell phone...I walked a little faster to get past it all...It began to rain and I inhaled the heavy ozone smell...The sounds of cars moving through the water reminded me of a sword cutting through the air in slow motion...

....

...I could see her clearly even from a good distance, for the moon was full and illuminated the street with its deep glow. She was looking casually into the sombre river flowing gently under the High Gate bridge. A murder of crows pecked at the remains of another bird and several dogs roamed around the riverbanks, providing contrast in an otherwise picturesque scene. When she saw me approaching her indifferent glare turned to a mischievous grin.

-I knew you would make it. I uncovered some new information. Do you want to have a drink?

-Do I have a choice? I said trying hard to sound funny. She looked at me and laughed.

-You're buying tonight because I'm bringing you info.

-Sure, no problem...Smoke?

-Might as well make it a habit.

We decided to stop at the Crucible, a relatively quiet bar at the far end of the Market. A handful of early evening drinkers stole glances at us as we worked our way to a booth at the back. Sandra didn't waste any time getting to the point, something I was getting used to.

-It's amazing what you find out once you put your pick in the ground. I think I stumbled onto the biographer while I was re-reading an old paper about Mantra. By chance, do you recognize the name William Pawel?

I shook my head. Sandra looked disappointed at my reaction.

-He's a former university professor of literature and a purveyor of rare books. The rumour in academic circles is that he's something of a deviant, but who knows? Pawel is the only person to have written a full-length study on Mantra Hand's works.

-Why would that mean anything?

-The book was published only a few weeks after Mantra disappeared.

-That could just be a big fucking coincidence.

-Sure, but this study shows that both of them share a deep interest in the esoteric. Pawel drew comparisons between Mantra and Fulcanelli, the French alchemist who vanished before his two greatest works were published...Does it seem like a coincidence now?

I said nothing for a few moments and sipped the double scotch I ordered, my mind stuffy with shards and fragments. Looking at Sandra, her eyes seemed to tell me that we were on the right track, but on the right track to what exactly?

-In answer to your question, no, it doesn't seem like a coincidence, but finding Pawel isn't going to tell us if Mantra Hand is alive. Besides, that wasn't my assignment.

Sandra looked disappointed.

-Look, I don't know why you've suddenly lost interest but I think it's worth following up on.

-Do you want me to tell the Director you want out?

-You would like that, wouldn't you?

A grin a mile wide lit up her cherubic face. She leaned

in, kissing me lightly on the lips.

-I don't know why, but I like you...Maybe it's just because you love Mantra Hand as much as I do. Anyway, all this work would go faster if we made this a team effort, don't you think?

-Maybe.

-Which one of us is going to track down Mr. Pawel?

-I'll do it.

-Good. So where do we go from here?

-What do you mean?

-Your place or mine tonight?

-Are you willing to leave the walls of the city and head to the Outskirts?

She leaned in again and stuck her tongue in my mouth, the taste of cherry on her lips mixed with the smokiness of the 15 year scotch I was drinking.

-I guess that answers your question.

-Where do you see this going, Sandra?

She paused for a moment to think.

-All the way to the end.

Riddles

...Daylight

The traces of last night's dream wash away: images of tropical flowers and palm trees along the coast of an unknown paradise. I'm on a boat slipping away from the shore, moving over the Marianas Trench. I fall silently into the water, trying not to struggle, hoping there is a way to see the bottom of what is seemingly bottomless. The pressure from above crushes me as I sink further, my limp body settling into the dark...

As I write, I imagine that this is what Hell is really like; an eternity spent floating through a void without ever sensing the presence of another human being. However, Hell can also be salvation. Looking out the window at the heaving sea, an incurable nausea sets in. I open a window. The salty air hits my lungs and I nearly vomit.

....

-Checking out, sir? Did you enjoy your stay?

-Yes, very much, thank you for asking.

The woman's face, so idle and joyful, could only be that of an angel. I cast my head down and look at my worn shoes.

-How far is the train station from here? I ask in a whisper.

-About three kilometres. Shall I call you a cab, sir?

-No need. I'll walk.

I carry six items in addition to my small suitcase: a lighter, cigarettes, a pen, a journal, a wallet full of cash and credit, and a small knife. Stepping out onto the sun-washed sidewalk, I head down the path that leads from the hotel. I take one last look at the lounge, telling myself not to turn back for fear I may turn into a pillar of salt. Old scripture dies hard. In the distance, the labyrinthine streets await me.

....

In the Market Square.

Wandered for hours with no purpose other than to outrun my thoughts. I never did find the train station; perhaps I'm not ready to leave just yet. Twilight. An old man once told me that twilight is a dangerous time to be alone, as that is when sorcerers are at their strongest...In Sunday school the nuns told me to be wary of false prophets and men who summon the Devil...Perhaps the truth lies somewhere between the two extremes, the two halves; between why and when; action and inertia; life and death...I wish the nuns would have told me to be wary of women. Everything leads back to them, the women. When I left Ophelia that night so many eons ago, I had the feeling that despite my actions I had struck a nerve within her and I would soon hear from her again. My intuition proved correct as the phone rang a few days later.

"M. can I see you?"

"When? I'm kind of busy at the moment." I said it to see if she would beg.

"When it's convenient for you. I've had a lot on my mind since the other night."

"Good thoughts? Or more of the same? In other words, are you sharpening that knife as we speak?"

She didn't respond.

"Come by tomorrow night and we can get reacquainted, if you like."

I could hear muffled weeping on the end of the line.

"I'll be waiting for you, Ophelia."

Hanging up the phone, I sat back in my chair and cracked my knuckles, grinning from ear to ear. I drank some wine and smoked a little opium, gently laughing at the ceiling in a thick haze, imagining her cool flesh against mine. The flesh that I owned...

I pick up my few belongings and keep moving as night is falling fast; darkness is the tranquilizer. The smell of coffee permeates the air. Backgammon players argue and chatter endlessly. In the narrow lightless corners I pass, women dance behind veils as drums pound. Slowly, slowly, a tepid rhythm, building to crescendo, then BANG. I stop. I listen.

A radio is on and I hear the sermon: 'The first angel sounded his trumpet, and there came fire mixed with blood.' Can't see. A blur. Dizzy. The world spins away...

....

The call to prayer woke me this morning as thousands of people knelt toward Mecca. How I got to the train station is beyond my grasp. It's difficult to move. Sweat. The horizon appears black. What time is it? I never did have a watch, did I? The memory of *them* is an open wound. I hear more drums, and flutes. Note upon note fading. The scents of jasmine, roses, and hyacinths fill my nose, but I don't see any. A dog howls.

-Sir? I just wanted to inform you that the train is running a little late.

-Have you come to take me away?

-I'm just informing you that your train is running late. Do you need some water? You look a little pale.

-Sure, sure, thank you kindly.

He passes me a cup. The water is slightly dark, but I drink it down.

-Are there any other passengers?

-Excuse me, sir?

-Is anyone else boarding?

-Of course, but only a handful from what I can see. May I see your ticket?

I hand him the stub and he examines it closely, his eyes are bloodshot.

-Is everything in order?

He nods in agreement and walks off, whistling out of tune. I pull out my journal.

...Yes, I felt as though I owned her, and she wanted to be owned for she had no one else. Nothing felt greater than knowing I held dominion over her. She arrived that evening looking rather lifeless when I opened the door. Throwing her arms around my neck, she dug her dirty fingernails into my skin.

"I've missed you so much M.! Why did you leave me?"

I looked her in the eyes and smiled.

"To show you who I am, Ophelia."

She appeared puzzled by my words, but she made herself comfortable on my couch, reaching instantly for the wine I

73

had poured, taking it all down in one long gulp.

"Did you miss me at all, M.?"

"I rarely miss people, Ophelia. In our lives people come and go according to unknown laws, so what's the point of missing someone?"

She bit her fingernails and tossed back a lock of hair, casting her eyes down. Sitting beside her I caressed her stockinged thighs, planting my lips on her thin white neck.

"If anything, Ophelia I've missed your flesh."

Her body resisted me at first, but as my hands touched the cold surface of her skin she began to thaw. We fucked for hours that night, passively taking hits of opium in-between my ejaculations. In the end, we sat together on the couch, naked, sharing a cigarette, our minds and our bodies numb.

"Can we chat?"

"You can talk if you wish, I won't stop you."

"Did I ever tell you how I came to live in Midtown?"

"No, I don't think you did. You're a runaway, aren't you?"

She looked at me intensely while I snuffed out the cigarette.

"How did you know that, M.?"

"It's that obvious, Ophelia. The cutting, the need for

security, etcetera. All of that paints a picture of someone desperately in need of love."

"Have you ever loved anyone M.? It almost seems impossible."

I walked to the window and lit a fresh cigarette.

"I won't admonish you for making such a statement, Ophelia, so you realize that I'm not a total monster, but yes I believe I have loved someone."

"Is it me?" she asked squeamishly.

"Don't be stupid, Ophelia. We share nothing more than each other's bodies. The fact that we're having this conversation about love surprises me."

"I think I'm pregnant, M."

My eyes are closed. Those words still echo across unknown zones to reach me. Ha ha. The prospect of being a father was the furthest thing from my mind. In fact, I know it would never be possible with someone like Ophelia. Red is another story...Red was a pink sky turned gold and back again. Ophelia was the graveyard of a thousand colourless deaths.

"What do you mean, you think you're pregnant? With my child?" I said calmly.

"I haven't bled in a very long time, M. There has been no one else but you. I can almost feel its growth."

"This cannot happen, you know that. I mean really, Ophelia, do what you will but I'm washing my hands of this."

She smashed the wine glass and got up from the couch, her hands shaking. All I could do was laugh at her attempt at being assertive. I smoked casually as she trembled and eventually dropped the stem of the glass on the floor. I patted her head as her tears fell on my feet.

"You know an abortion would be for the collective good, right?" I said with feigned compassion.

She looked up at me through her tangled hair and let out a barely audible "Yes."

"Life is complicated enough as it is without throwing in more chaos. I'll even give you the money to have it done."

"You would do that?"

"Of course I would. As I said I'm not a total monster in the grand scheme, for there are always bigger monsters."

We got dressed and sat out on the balcony. The air was warm and the landscape of Midtown displayed a rare beauty. Ophelia absently ran her fingers over her womb. For a moment she possessed that glow that they say expecting mothers have, staring off into the brightly lit horizon, then it faded.

"You're right M., this is not a world for a child to live in."

"You see what I see, don't you?"

"Yes, I think I do."

...Yes I think I do, I think I do, think I do, I do, I.

-Sir, the train has arrived, do you have any extra luggage?

-.....?

-Sorry to startle you...the train has arrived.

-Yes, yes, thank you...Thank you very much.

He walks off in a blur of motion. I'm tired and I hope that my berth is comfortable. Where am I going anyway? Ahh, yes...further up the coast...anywhere will do...Maui, Spain, the Cayman Islands.

Overall it doesn't matter.

Anywhere I go the world will absorb me like a maggot absorbs dead flesh, or a honey bee pollen. I'm free...
-All aboard! All aboard! Last call.

....

Night. Deep and black. Only the glow from the tiny lamp sheds light upon my hands. Too hot. I turn away from the window and blow out more smoke. My hand nearly snaps the pencil, but I continue... "The maker doesn't want it, the buyer doesn't use it, and the user doesn't see it. What is it?" Those were the words Red greeted me with when I rang her, hours after Ophelia calmly left my apartment.
"Can we talk, Red?"
"Over the phone, or in person?"
"Hopefully in person."
"First you have to answer the riddle."
"I don't have time for this, Red."
"Really? That's too bad, because it seems like you are the one desperate to talk and not the other way around."
"I see your bitchiness is shining through nicely."
"I'm hanging up now..."

"No, wait. Let me think about it."

"Once you figure it out, then we can talk. Get back to me."

Fuck her. Pacing the room I grew agitated. Two cigarettes, then a third and fourth. Sweat. Thoughts overlapped and spun and grew out of control until I cursed her up and down. Then I remember laughing. She knew she had me in her grip, which I was unwilling to admit. My living room became a disaster area as I plumbed book upon book for an answer. To my surprise the Internet also let me down. I sat on my couch and watched the cigarette ash burn down to my fingers...I felt nothing. I was numb.

The lights in the hallway of the train car have dimmed. Maybe I can still get a drink in the dining car before I slip out of consciousness. Sleep. Dear, dear sleep how I miss you. I amble from car to car until I see the dim incandescence of Paradise, and St. Peter himself serving drinks behind the counter.

-Still time for a round before lights out?

-What will you have? he says almost in a whisper.

-Double scotch, neat. Can I smoke in here?

He nods and flicks open a gold plated Zippo, then sets down my scotch.

-You are most kind. Nothing like a drink and a smoke before bed.

-Where are you headed, sir, if you don't mind me asking?

-To the end of the line. I'm meeting someone there...or hoping to meet them there.

-Is she expecting you?

-What makes you think it's a she?

-It's always a she.

I down my scotch and laugh. He smiles knowing he's right. His eyes seem to glow as his grin disappears. Tap, tap, another. I put up three fingers for a triple.

-Is this your last one, sir?

I look at him closely, baring my teeth.

-Hopefully.

....

A deep whistle wakes me from the dream. When did I come back here? Red's smoldering eyes behind the mask...lips, tongue...body entwined in worlds of dreamland legs, her silence rising up to the heavens like prayers do. I lay in a pool of sweat. Morning already? Too bright...Have to pull the blind down...I close my eyes and attempt to catch some remnant of what I saw. No luck. I sit up, slip a cigarette into my mouth and breathe in my slow death. I shake my pen and wake it from its slumber.

...Numb, as though a dagger of ice had run up my back. I remember leaving my apartment that night, desperately racking my brain for the answer. I'll show her, I thought. I needed her challenge as much as I needed my hand tugging the chain metaphorically wrapped around Ophelia's neck. The night air did nothing to calm me, neither did the gently flowing river near the High gate bridge, or the soft hues of the gaslights leading to the Observatory. As I continued toward the Marble Corridor I came upon the Great Cemetery and decided to walk among the dead—I always hoped they would whisper their secrets to me from the beyond. I heard nothing, but as I stood in the moonlight staring at the fresh earth over a new grave, I felt the answer to the riddle spark in my brain. I ran all the way back to my apartment, out of breath as I dialed her number. No answer. Her answering machine came on but I couldn't even speak...What a moment. I had found the key to her lock but I didn't find the words. To imagine paradise is to have faith beyond words, even in the midst of total darkness, but it was the darkness that led me to the answer and I have never forgotten that.

I put my pen down. A bitter memory far removed, dissolving too fast for me to taste one last time for good measure. Opening the blind I feel the heat of the burgeoning day hit my face through the dirty window. I pull out my knife and turn the blade toward the light, which illuminates tiny flecks of blood. I can't help but smile. I run the flat of the blade across my tongue...
Ever closer.

Mask

When I woke the next day, I looked out the bedroom door and saw Sandra wrapped in my housecoat. I watched her for a few moments; caught in contemplation, she was drinking a cup of coffee and flipping through my copy of The Black Roses. When she looked up she met my gaze with a smile.

-Spying on me? I took the liberty of making coffee.

-Not at all.

-You're late for work again, you know.

I looked at my watch and felt another pang of nausea. Sandra seemed unconcerned. Her attention was directed solely to the pages of Mantra Hand, and she bit her upper lip as she read in silence, taking occasional sips of my Jamaican Blue Mountain brew. I didn't bother to move fast, maybe because I wanted to digest (again) the events that had taken place between me and Sandra. Either that or I just wanted to bask in her essence a little longer. Eventually I grabbed myself a

83

steaming cup of coffee and when I sat down beside her; she slammed the book shut.

-You're not going to be the one to go in to work today.

-Excuse me? Why?

-Have you forgotten your assignment already? You have to find William Pawel.

-What are you going to do, then?

-Well, go in to work of course. I mean, one of us has to keep up appearances.

-Finding Pawel might take some time that we don't have.

She leaned toward me and placed my hand on her left breast which I gently squeezed. Sandra grinned and gave me a peck on the cheek. Our bodies still carried the aroma of sex.

-Don't worry so much. We have nothing but time. Just call the Director and tell him you decided to hand the assignment over to me and then you can take a few days off to track down Pawel.

A pang of uncertainty ran through me, but I picked up the phone and made the call, feeling it was the only thing to do at this point. There was no turning back. When the Director answered he issued an icy flow of words, asking me why I wasn't at work and why I wanted to hand the assignment over so suddenly after taking such a keen interest in the material.

-I'm feeling a little run down, sir. I think I'm in need of a little time off. You were right in saying that Sandra would make a fine replacement on this project...I'll leave it in her capable hands for the moment.

-Sounds like a wise decision. See to it that you're in fine shape once you return so we don't run into this situation again, understand?

-Yes, sir. No problem.

-Oh, and let Sandra know that the assignment is hers. I want her up to speed before she comes back into the office.

I froze.

-...I'll send her an email, I said slowly.

-Good, good. I'm sure she'll be enthused about the project, don't you?

-Uhh, yeah...Very enthused.

-Excellent. I'll be seeing you then, take care.

Setting down the receiver, I turned and saw Sandra smoking one of my cigarettes. The bathrobe had disappeared and her flesh was on full display across my couch—tiny wisps of smoke curled into the air, a subtle grin on her crimson lips.

-So are you going to fuck me one more time before I leave?

-I have a choice, right?

-Of course you do, but don't make the wrong one.

-Would fucking you again be the wrong one? I said jokingly.

-Only one way to find out, right?

She sat up and put out the cigarette. Spreading her legs, she slid her fingers lightly over her pubis, and cupped a breast with the other hand.

-Don't keep me waiting, she whispered.

....

She slipped away. I didn't even notice, probably because I fell asleep again. When I looked outside the sky was becoming overcast, and my apartment seemed cold without Sandra to warm it with me. *The Black Roses* lay turned over on the couch. Sandra had shown such a keen interest in it earlier in the day that I decided to sit down and peruse its pages again. I smiled when I realized her lace panties lay beneath Mantra Hand's words. I grabbed them and moved them through my hands, remembering how I took them off with my teeth. I was forgetting who I was; the situation with Sandra had progressed so quickly that my mind needed to play catch up. As I was about to open the book, the phone rang from a number I didn't recognize.

-Hello?

-It's me.

-Marion?! Where are you? More importantly, where have you been?

-I'm in the hospital. Will you come and see me?

-Of course! What happened to you? It's been months...

-We'll talk more later...come soon. I'm in the R wing at Midtown General. Bye.

Her sudden call took me by surprise, but finding out she was in the R Wing was nothing new. My heart felt cold. I pictured myself in the not so distant past making numerous calls to her apartment...I had even resorted to sitting across the street by the Vai Soli fountain, hoping to catch a glimpse of her passing by her window...I sent letters, getting no response. Night always seems to bloom early when she calls, and the air feels colder. A dull current of dread moved through my body when I put the receiver back in its cradle. So much can change from one moment to the next... I became dizzy and closed my eyes, wondering if her face had changed since I saw her last. I cursed out loud and then swallowed a couple Ativans I had been prescribed for work anxiety. I stepped out onto the balcony, looking at Midtown shrouded comfortably in the distance by heavy fog, and my stomach felt tangled again.

....

As the train glided toward the Marble Corridor, the skies opened up. The closer I got to the hospital, the harder the rain seemed to fall, yet once I entered the doors into the R Wing a dense silence welcomed me. Hospitals are dreary places; full of stranded ghosts and the infirm, we walk through the halls looking for loved ones among so much death, hoping that we will find them well...Midtown Hospital still had a large nursery that you could look into and see all the fresh, half-blind faces, beautiful and red cheeked...But if you walked a little further down the hall, the icy gleam of the morgue stood before you with its subtle smell of a million lost lives. A reminder of our beginnings and endings, full circle, alpha and omega. I've often asked God to let me find death elsewhere: a darkened alley after a heavy rainfall, a park bench, the subway, even my own home amongst my books - but never in a hospital. The closer I got to finding Marion, the dimmer the lights seemed to get.

I thought about how the mentally ill are always tucked away, as though the mind is less important than the body that houses that invisible, strange entity we call consciousness.

No one took notice of me. Or if they did, I may have appeared as something else to them: a man on fire, a KGB agent, a potted plant...Anything but myself. A man drooling out the side of his mouth looked at me, and speaking in a drugged drawl said "Will it bleed? I see it bleed." His eyes drifted over me before resting on the ceiling. I felt my face go flush; not because I was afraid, but because the words he spoke seemed familiar in an obscure way. When I finally made it to Marion's room, it was like entering a tomb.

-You came like you said you would.

I sat down and looked at her closely...a dullness had overtaken her since the last time I had seen her.

-When I heard your voice it almost didn't seem real. I thought you were dead, calling from beyond.

She stifled a laugh then frowned.

-Not dead, but confused. Do you have a cigarette?

-You can't smoke in here.

-We're going to take a stroll. The weather looks perfect.

The fog appeared to have thickened.

-Let's go then.

We walked slowly through the quiet halls. What surprised me was how radiant she appeared. It was as though being on the fringe of death brought out a deep glow. She looked at me with curiosity.

-Something has happened to you recently. I can tell. You seem less tense. It's a woman, isn't it?

I said nothing and she stared at me with a girlish delight.

-It is a woman! What has she done to you?

-What do you mean?

-So you don't deny it, then?

-No. We met at work and we share a common interest in Mantra Hand.

She took a long pull on her cigarette.

-I started to have bad dreams again, you know? One of

the reasons I disappeared was because I thought a change of scenery might clean up the attic. It didn't. The dreams persisted and I thought of you, so I came back.

-That doesn't sound like you at all. Since when did you take me into consideration?

-You would be surprised at how much I think about you. Why didn't we ever make it, hmm?

I wasn't sure if the question was rhetorical so I remained silent, even though a part of me desired her and the broken pieces she carried within herself. We grabbed some coffee from the cafeteria and sat on the benches outside, soaking in the burgeoning fog.

-What are these dreams you're having about?

-They have a very dark, almost cinematic feel to them. They're very vivid. There's always a man in them who reminds me of you, yet he looks nothing like you at all..He's more imposing, not large or overly tall...a strange energy surrounds him, and I always seem to meet him somewhere obscure or hidden - places that would only exist in a world gone mad. He's always

92

trying to seduce me, but I'm afraid. Then, without fail, another woman appears.

-Another woman? Do you recognize her?

She looked at me grimly.

-No, but she has dark hair - crimson - and a nice shape. When she sees me in his arms she slits his throat and he bleeds all over me. I've never seen her face, only the edge of the knife coming toward me next, and then I wake up.

-And this man reminds you of me? What about the woman? Who does she remind you...

-I don't want to talk about it anymore.

She flicked her cigarette into the fog and turned away from me.

-They affect you that much...I'm sorry.

-I'm being released in a couple days. You should come see me at my apartment then. We can talk more or whatever. I need a rest right now. I'm sorry.

She said all this with her back turned to me, barely audible as though the congesting dense air around us was stealing her voice.

I looked at my watch, realizing I had to leave.

-Whatever you do, don't come empty handed when you decide to visit.

I was confused by her instructions, because she had seemed desperate to see me when we talked on the phone. I placed a hand on her shoulder and felt a deep chill emanating from her, even through the sweater she was wearing.

-Don't get lost in the fog.

-I won't. Do you need another cigarette?

She turned slightly and eked out a smile.

-Thanks. I look forward to your visit...Really.

As I walked away from her, the fog became oppressive. After a few steps, I looked over my shoulder to where we had been sitting and all I could see was opaqueness. Pulling up my collar, I treaded carefully as I disappeared into the streets.

....

Nights in Midtown, particularly around the Dragon Court or the Waterfront Market, consist of the sounds of suppressed screams, occasional smears of blood, and the ever present smell of opium in the air which create a sense of disorientation. That night when I left the hospital was no different. I took the subway to the edge of the Dragon Court and decided to grab a drink at one of the many run down watering holes in the Pavilion Arcade. Only one lounge was open: The Arcana. As I stepped into the foyer with dark green lights, a woman emerged in a mask made of thick plaster, an iridescent blue butterfly meticulously painted upon it. Her eyes matched the phantom colour perfectly, and they looked deeply into me. I turned to go.

-What's your hurry? she whispered.

-I was looking for someone and they're not here.

-You didn't even look inside, so how would you know?

-Just a lucky guess.

She placed her hand on my shoulder. Her fingers tickled the skin on my neck.

-Now, now, no need to be shy. Come in for a drink.

I hesitated for a moment, but the glow of her eyes drew me forward and I followed her into a large, vacant room. Sparsely furnished, the room boasted immaculate dark mahogany panelling, a well-polished bar, and various paintings by Magritte, Dali, and Mondrian. She led me to a chair and then disappeared into the back. Sweating uncontrollably, I reached inside my coat for my Ativans and popped a couple into my mouth. Being in that semi-dark space put me in a strange mood and all the events of late flooded my mind in torrents. Three masked women walked into the room, taking up positions at various points: one stood at the bar, one stopped at a large card table, and the third reclined on a blue crushed velvet couch.

-Can I bring you a drink, love?

I was startled by her voice; Butterfly had returned without notice. I was drenched in perspiration. My heart raced as she traced her soft fingers over my brow...I could feel a tiny smile beneath her mask.

-Uh...sure...scotch, neat...and some water please.

-Are you not feeling well? she said in a mock motherly

tone.

-Just water, please...

-The scotch is on the house.

-Wha...I don't understand...

-Courtesy of our patron.

-Who would that be?

She refused to answer, as though it were a matter of utmost privacy. Instead, she walked over to the bar and whispered to the woman there, who soon came over to hand me my drink. As she approached I could see that her mask depicted a lion's head, while her skin appeared dark orange in the eerie glow. She sat down across from me.

-Butterfly tells me you're looking for someone. Were you supposed to meet them here? This is a private establishment and I know I've never seen you before.

-I think I've been misunderstood...I was just out...

-Walking?

-Yes...exactly.

-It's odd how you stumbled upon our little palace without an invitation.

-I was invited in.

-Hmmm...Well, I suppose that changes everything.

-How so?

-Come over to the card table with me.

-Can I smoke in here? I asked breathlessly.

-*Everything* is permitted here.

I downed the scotch and quickly lit a cigarette before slowly following Lioness to the card table where a shapely woman, masked in the image of a swan, sat calmly, her well-manicured hands sifting through a tarot deck.

-You look tense, my dear. Have another drink, on us.

I slid into a chair. My hands gripped my thighs tightly, and the ash began to fall from the cherry of my smoke. I accepted their gesture despite myself, attempting to drown the inherent fear that my drinks were being cut with something without my knowledge. One should never trust women in masks. Swan could sense my discomfort.

-What are you thinking about so intently?

What *was* I thinking?

-Water. The Seine, the Liffey, the Thames, the Volga...leading out into the vast dark sea, and a small boat floating on slightly churning waves.

Butterfly set another scotch in front of me and Swan motioned for me to drink.

-Hmmm, very profound. Shall I do a reading for you?

I nodded, despite being unsure of the method, and watched her turn the cards

-The Magician, the Hermit reversed, the High Priestess, King of Pentacles, the Moon.

-Is that good, bad, what? I asked somewhat indifferently.

She looked at me in silence, as though I should intuitively know the hidden meaning of the cards. I turned my face away, feeling like a large weight had been placed upon me. The glare of the lamps seemed to intensify and I felt weak. The room began to spin as Butterfly's voice warbled in my ears.

-Your answer lies here. Relax, change, shed your skin. Then nothing. Fade out. Black.

When I opened my eyes again, I was in my bed, alone. Sitting up I could see the sun peeking over the horizon, as though the past day's experiences had been a dream. I rubbed my eyes and fell back on the pillow wondering what the fuck had happened. Pulling the covers over my head, I didn't move for the rest of the day.

The Mysterious Gate

The sun, looking as old as it does bright, creeps in through the shade; the train has reached its destination. Silence. Two more cigarettes. If I close my eyes I see beyond the train, beyond buildings...two rivers lead to a blackened ocean, the godless mass of water. Doors open while others close...tall grass...honeybees...fireflies, and wild geese flying south. Then nothing. A knock...

-We have arrived sir. Is everything okay? Shall I call the porter?

-No need. I will be departing shortly.

...No two spiders spin the same web, though being a curious insect I became caught in the web that Red had spun just for me. I practically ran to her that night from the cemetery, oblivious to all else around me, acting like a teenager pining for affection. The lamp in the window was on and I could see her shadowy outline behind the curtains. She met me at the door wearing the apocalyptic mask upon her face, only the dim glow of her eyes visible in the moonlight.

-Do you have an answer for me? she asked in a soft tone.

-Yes! A coffin my dear, a coffin.

Stepping aside she let me in and told me to make myself comfortable, making it very clear she would summon me at her leisure. I sat limply on the couch, out of breath and elated, and I smiled. A bottle of whiskey was open on the table so I fixed a stiff drink for myself and downed it in a single draught.

-Come up the stairs slowly.

Her voice was like a spectre speaking through the aether. As I climbed the stairs Piranesi's 'Imaginary Prisons' greeted me along the walls, evenly spread out in a wave of black drawbridges, platforms, and bas-reliefs creating a complex

101

maze of dead ends and chasms. Her door was slightly ajar as I reached the landing, and a stream of blue light seeped through.

-I'm here.

She lay naked upon the bed, with the exception of the wonderful mask upon her face. Getting up she seemed to drift to me, putting her arms around my neck. Sweet peppermint. Alabaster skin. The deep blue glow enveloped us as we clawed at one another until she forced me down and climbed on top of me, moving in a deep rhythm until we both came...

Removing the mask, she placed a single kiss on my lips and spoke into my eyes.

-Checkmate. Bang, you're dead.

....

I move my fingers to my lips and feel only the dry and cracked skin. Too hot to write or breathe. Drinks are what I need, and plenty of them, somewhere in the deep shade of this new city that looks so much like the last. I must depart and go look at the sea, for the heat is making mirages in my head. Vultures look like angels far off in the sky...or maybe it is just a plane falling to earth in the form of a comet...I hear her say in that raw graceful tone, quoting Dante: "When our intellect is drawing close to its desire, its paths are so profound memory cannot follow where it goes."

round and round and round the words go

round and round to nowhere

I laugh as I make my way into the blazing sun, where all the phantoms flit around. The hum is almost deafening. Another cigarette. Sunglasses. My kingdom for a drink... I can see the ocean so clearly...so much clearer and calmer than my view from the hotel, or the lounge, or anywhere...even in my dreams. The sun burns my face in the same way those memories do. Red told me a secret that night and I can only liberate myself from it through ink...And blood.

-"Do you want to know something?" she whispered into my ear.

-"Anything," I replied without hesitation.

-"There isn't much time left."

-"Time?"

She smiled. An indescribable smile, like the Mona Lisa.

-"When I look at the sky these days, I don't find pleasure in the blue."

-"Well what do you find pleasure in?" I asked while moving my index finger across her naked back.

-"Something larger than pleasure, more eerie, unspoken."

I pulled my finger away and lit a cigarette, which she promptly took from my hand, easing her way above the sheets and caressing the surface of the mask.

-"Well then it must be death, since it's the negation of the pleasure principle."

-"My, you're smarter than you look. You also don't fuck too badly either, which is something of a surprise to me."

-"Ha. You really are a bitch."

-"If only you knew."

-"I'm beginning to see that you get what you want when you want it."

-"You've only just discovered that now," she said plainly.

-"Even though I'm not voicing my ideas it doesn't mean I don't have them."

-"Well, what else do you see, then? What can you tell me about myself that I don't already know?"

I looked at her intently, searching the void of her face...Her eyes told me nothing, it was as though she could switch on a mechanism that blanketed her soul. And the harder I looked the more I became disheartened. What was I expecting?

She turned over and laughed to herself.

....

As the daylight is extinguished, the night brings little comfort. Looking out onto the cold, indifferent water, I watch the last vestiges of the sun's rays disappear. I took a small room up the road, away from the steady hum of the city. There are so many moons and so much space between us...June rain...the dead ends appear...Why haven't I seen you in the street or on the train? Wishful, empty thinking...I look for your shadow. Off in the distance I see two lovers part on the beach, a deep longing on their suntanned faces, each one straining not to move away from the other. I grimace and slam my drink down on the table, a sick twist in my stomach as the woman strides toward the road, her dark hair flowing in the gentle breeze. It makes me sick.

Shaking my head as I light another cigarette, my thoughts turn from a desert heat to a tundra cold...winter sets in and the snow falls as the seasons of my day quickly turn. There are too many women about. I can see them all through the stained window, walking toward the water to drown, laughing all the way like a band of crazed nymphs or sprites, I can't decide which. Wishful, empty thinking. I look for your shadow on the pages.

....

"Did you know that the largest single flower is the Rafflesia or 'corpse flower'?"

I turned away from the window. The sun was blazing, even though it was nearly September..the heat on my face.

"What was that, Red?"

"Have you ever seen a corpse flower up close?"

"No. I've never been to that part of the world."

"I remember seeing one once in the rainforest. It's a beautiful specimen that reeks of decaying flesh."

"I'll bet you enjoyed that smell."

She looked at me slyly.

"You may be right. I should give you more credit. Come sit with me" she said, patting the cushion.

Leaning in close, as though she were going to kiss my face, she spoke softly.

"Nothing is as beautiful as an ending. Remember that. Everything in between is just a lead up to an even greater mystery we can't touch."

She put her slender fingers on my lips and I kissed them gently.

"Where did you come from Red?" I asked suddenly.

"I barely remember anymore, it's been so long."

"But you do remember, right?"

"Maybe...But I know where I'm going. Will you follow me?"

"That depends on how dangerous the terrain is."

"It's very dangerous. You may never come back."

"Somewhere in the back of my mind I think that may not matter," I said bitterly.

"We'll see."

....

I can't sleep, the air is too still. The world is too still. Did she warn me of that? I'm trying to remember, but my memory is usually a failure unless it's about *them*. The pages pile up but the words hardly seem real. I hear a tapping at my window, but I don't bother to look. Perhaps I fear what might be there, though it must be the wind, right? That's what I keep telling myself. What else could it be? Demons? No, no, only in my dreams. If they were faces of the dead at least that I could smile at. I need fresh air and the words of Prospero... "The cloud-capped towers, the gorgeous palaces, the solemn temples, the great globe itself, Yea, all which it inherit, shall dissolve."

I smell the night blooming like a Casablanca Lily or blood from a wound. The hotel is as mute as a tomb as I walk out the doors to greet the full moon, and as I look to the ocean, I see the deep light from above caress the waves. It's then that I see her, off in the distance, watching the motion of gentle currents. Her hair is different than before, and she walks nimbly, without a care in the world. A full moon will do that to a person. I follow her. For a moment I wonder where her lover is, then just as quickly put him out of my mind. He had the appearance of one of those overly suave playboys that I paint all with the same brush: useless. He doesn't realize what a wonderful woman he has, though that is typical of us men: never recognizing the value of a good catch. Ha, what the hell am I saying? Would I have ever made such a comment to Red? She would have laughed in my face. Still, one can imagine a million possibilities without actually taking hold of any of them. The woman heads toward the city, not even looking over her shoulder to see if a cab is available or if she is being followed. Yet...there is more to be done, more bridges to cross, much, much more. I'm a long way from home. All the better. No one will ever know. The city lies quiet as the shade of night is pulled down. Nothing can touch me now, as I reach the gates to the other side. But the other side of what? Even I don't know where I will tread, but I know how it ends. I scribble what is left of my memories and drift into the night...

She passed me a glass of wine. Summer seemed to be fading away fast, and her hair appeared more crimson than it had before. I looked at the clock: 11:11pm. Red was trying to convince me to do mescaline with her.

-Why in God's name do you want me to do that? Not that I'm saying no, exactly.

-It's the doorway to the Muted Horn...

I snickered.

-Are you mocking me, or are you really as sceptical as I think you are?

Downing my wine, I managed a smile.

-So what you're telling me, though I'm not sure you're telling me anything at all, is that the Muted Horn is metaphorical, not actual...

-Not at all. The Muted Horn is a way of communication, of connection to consciousness. Have you ever read the Tibetan Book of the Dead?

-No. Does that mean something?

-Is everything a series of pointless questions with you? Do you want to see the Horn or not?

-Sure...Yeah...But is there any other way?

-Of course, but this one is the most interesting. You don't want to disappoint me, do you?

She had the buttons in her hand...I hadn't even seen her produce them, it was as though they simply appeared in her palm. I took three and began to chew one of the fibrous buttons, her eyes on me the whole time. She pressed her wet lips to mine before placing one of them on her tongue.

-How long is this going to last?

-Ten hours maybe...give or take.

-We're in for a ride hey? I said with a hint of nervousness.

She didn't answer, but poured us each some more wine and began to chew her second button. My mouth had begun to go numb. She took my hand and placed it on her cleavage, and took a deep breath...I began to chew my other two buttons...sweat...I remember lots of sweat, as though the earth was on fire and I stood in the middle with Red.

-Just relax...it's going to take some time for us to elevate. You'll see the Horn, I promise you...

The curvature of her breasts, which I began kneading gently with my hands, seemed to melt beneath my fingers. I stopped. Red opened her eyes.

-Why did you stop? That felt sooooo good.

-You look different.

I said it with conviction, even though I wasn't sure I saw anything change in her features. She placed my hands back on her breasts and stuck her tongue in my mouth, which tasted like wine and chocolate.

-Relax, relax...why are you always so tense...

Her mouth was on my neck sucking at my dry flesh in a frenzy. Minutes went by...hours?

No...seconds? Blue and green and yellow light. Yessssssss... a melding of colours, textures...garbled sounds...my own? Was she coming? Was I naked? Was she naked? Yes, yes...on the floor...my own teeth biting her taut white flesh. Screams. Passion or pain it didn't matter. Better if it was pain. I held her as though I were holding a beam of light.

-I know what you want Mantra...I know what you want...

My eyes couldn't focus on her. Nothing was in focus. Her voice seemed distant but she was right beneath me, her fingers digging into the flesh of my back.

-I know what you want...

My lips moved in response but no words came from my throat.

-Cut yourself Mantra, then bleed me.

My head was spinning, of that I'm sure...Am I? What am I sure of now? Ha ha ha Red...look at what you have helped to create. My hands shake. Bleed me bleed me bleed me. So insistent. How could I deny her, let alone myself? Pain seemed to be something I reserved for Ophelia, as I stood above her. Red's smile was like the Cheshire Cat, wide and strangely inviting. She wanted to lick the blade. Then I licked it, running the tip over my tongue.

-Slowly...not too deep...the buttons will start taking effect soon.

I held the knife gently in my palm, looking at the metallic sheen that appeared to grow brighter and brighter the longer I looked at it. Red became impatient.

-What are you waiting for? Just do it!

The knife fell from my hand, hovering in the air for an eternity before falling to the ground. I could see Red's lips move...just movement...no sound. Blue turned green, green turned gold, gold turned to blue again. Black ants moved in droves around our bodies. The walls melted in silence, the music warbled in my ears...

-Fuck, turn it off. Turn it the fuck off!

Red laughed and laughed, wisps of smoke blanketing her features. Where did the cigarette come from? She didn't move, did she? I can't remember...

-Do you see it yet, Mantra? Do you see what I see?

Tiny white spheres came through the aether in expansive lines, taking shape, but into what? The last words I heard her say...

-Follow me through the door, Mantra...Meet me on the other side.

....

I've watched her from a distance and I can't keep the smile from my face, knowing she is mine. The lover is nowhere to be found, and it's quite apparent by her knotted brow that she is worried. It's okay, I've been unable to move toward her much, for I've not found the energy to do so in this endless space of sand and heat. The Horn has been quiet as of late in this denseness. It has all come to this. She has such an elegant form...

There is only the barest flicker of light now. I see her shape, wavering and twisting.

Back home the leaves must be falling from the trees, painting the streets a dark orange. A scene I can only imagine, for I no longer desire to see it again. I shut my lids and smile, then open them and let the image fade. Grey light now. Her shape shimmers, almost glowing in the eerie growing penumbra. I smoke one last cigarette and blow the smoke toward heaven...I wave to her. Does she see me? Is she shielding her eyes to make out my face in failing light? It doesn't matter, I'm so very close, I can almost taste her now. Whispers, whispers, whispers. I ache for silence...She is sitting in the angel white sand with her toes in the water, which gleams and twinkles. Is anyone around? The whispers have died and the city has died and the only two people left are me and her, though she still doesn't look in my direction. Maybe she has been playing hard to get this whole time. Silly girl. Why would you do something like that to me? Someone who is no longer a stranger.

I raise the blade.

Encounters

...When I woke again, night had already descended. My head pounded. My stomach churned. The bed was soaked in sweat. My answering machine blinked. Two messages had been left during my deathly sleep. I didn't listen to them, believing they were both from Sandra. I took a bottle of whiskey out to the balcony, lit a cigarette, and looked out across the Midtown skyline, feeling as though a buzzsaw had been put through my mind. I drank for an hour, then passed out on my couch only to wake up again closer to morning. Another message had added itself to my machine. I hit the button almost unconsciously and listened with my eyes closed. It was Marion; her voice sounded hollow, and she spoke slowly.

"They're letting me go today. Maybe that's a bad idea, who knows. Anything is better than white walls right now, even if it's the gloom of Midtown. Shit, I find it hard to admit but I missed the grit and grime. Before long I'll be back to my old self...haha, yeah...Anyway, you know where to find me. I'll leave a candle in the window as a beacon. Later."

The Black Roses was still on the coffee table. I looked at it for a long time, feeling as though I was missing something. Turning over, I hit the message button to hear Sandra's voice again.

"Where are you? I'm just calling to say that this manuscript is a real jewel! I'm shocked that you let it go so easily. Was it my womanly charm? Well, if it was I can't blame you. Against my better judgement I'm sending you scans of a few of the later parts so you can have a gander. That'll be our little secret, okay? Maybe we can see each other soon."

A real jewel. I began to think she loved Mantra Hand more than anyone or anything. But how could she be in love with someone she had never met? I told myself that she was in love with his arrangement of words, his ideas, but that didn't make me feel any better about being away from her. Actually, it just aroused my curiosity enough for me to check if her email had arrived. The sun was peeking over the dull Midtown horizon as I printed the dozen or so pages. My eyes and stomach still ached, and I noticed the empty Ativan container. Fuck. I kept saying it over and over in my head until it lost all meaning. Tucking the pages under the cover of The Black Roses I poured whiskey into a flask and threw on my coat. The ride into the City was going to be a long one.

....

...The lights in the train car dimmed as I read, and the coldness of Mantra's words sent a frost over my mind. Opening my flask, I took a shot. No one was riding the train that early, but Mantra's fingers...his hand...seemed to grasp at me across time and space, as though he was tracing the steps I had taken along Salamander Road years before. Thinking of all the locations he mentioned in The Black Roses led me to believe that I had seen him before, shrouded in shadow or out of the corner of my eye. Was he ever that close? I read on...

(Absence)

There is only the barest flicker of light once you take a wrong turn and end up where I am (wherever that is), and sadly I've ended up where the bones of old memories are housed. The question is, how is that possible? By definition R. seemed to me, at least up close, a conglomeration of many women I knew from the past and present (future?), as though by some miracle or mysterious force my previous perceptions of women coalesced into one being. I began to think that my mind had begun a slow disintegration into nothingness, because no rational person can have these ideas and actually believe them. The Word was made flesh. Another interpretation is the flesh became the Word. R. never said much more on the subject of the Muted Horn, or for that matter Midtown's founders. Did she have some sort of connection to those long dead people? Sending messages through the untold depths of the Horn? In essence it doesn't really matter, for my intentions from the start had nothing to do with knowing more about her other connections, but rather with her untold depths. As we became more inseparable and our sexual adventures became more frequent, I began to see the layers that comprised her...With each passing caress I saw a series of different people burst through as though they were a part of one large hallucination. I didn't dare tell her this for fear of being mocked. Little did she know that as meek as I appeared in her eyes nothing would stop me from finding out who she was beneath the inflated charm. There were Others who shared the limelight with us, even though I'm unsure if she was aware of them. I direct the attention of the audience reading these words to another woman...

I chuckled to myself after reading that last sentence. There always seems to be another woman to complicate matters. I stared at the flask and realized Mantra Hand and I were really not that different. Downing the rest of the sour whiskey, images of Sandra and Marion blurred together. I threw the flask down the centre of the train car. Mantra Hand was a prick; a very intelligent prick, but a rotten prick nonetheless. A stalker, a creep. Maybe I wasn't much better...

....

The morning bloomed slowly. I spent two hours in a Chinese coffeehouse in the Dragon Court trying to sober myself, flipping through The Black Roses. Passage after passage illuminated the picture, but he was still so hard to see. I thought of Sandra underlining sentences and adding copious footnotes to the file, yet I felt as though I was ahead of her, running a race that had no finish line. My cell phone rang, just as I sipped the last of my coffee. It was Marion.

-I wasn't expecting to hear from you so soon.

-Are you in the City? You must be, I can hear voices in the background.

-Yeah, I'm in the Dragon Court...reading.

-Come see me.

-Now? I asked curiously.

-Did you get my message earlier?

-Yes. I was sleeping. I've been pretty worn out lately.

-The candle will be in the window.

-But why, it's morning...

-I'll see you soon.

I never seemed to get the last word. As I looked around,

the crowd of people began to file out, leaving me alone in a mental and physical vacuum. Rushing out, the cool air felt good on my face.

Sure enough there was a candle in the window. I stood outside for a while looking at it, thinking Mantra Hand had needed a candle to guide him through the Void. The guy was fucking crazy. Maybe we all were. When I looked up at Marion's window again, I saw her looking down at me as though she knew I would be there at that moment. I waved. She stared in bewilderment. The hallway to her apartment was a lot like the hospital: dead quiet. I didn't bother to knock, I just walked right in.

-You made it.

She was facing the window; the daylight oozed in. A cloud of smoke circled her head. A record played almost soundlessly. I couldn't place it. Sitting down across from her I threw my book on the floor.

-Yeah, I made it. It's already been a long morning.

-You look terrible. A lot worse than when you came to see me in the hospital.

-Thanks.

-Need anything? Water?

-Do you have any Ativans?

Marion looked at me with uncertainty. I didn't flinch.

-Sure, go crazy.

She tossed me the bottle. I downed four and laid back in the chair, staring at the ceiling.

-What are you reading here?

She picked The Black Roses off the floor and pulled out the loose pages.

-Those, Marion, are from the pen of Mantra Hand.

-So this is your big secret? Or is it that woman you're seeing?

-Neither. Both are a mystery to me. She's doing the archiving right now, probably as we speak.

She emailed these to me to look at.

-Even I know this kind of info shouldn't be outside of the walls of the Hall of Records, especially because it's so personal.

-Why did you ask me to come so urgently, Marion? I said, changing the subject.

-I wanted to continue where I left off the last time we saw each other. Are you up for that?

She could see my body turning to jelly from the drugs, but I nodded in agreement, even managing to slip a cigarette into my mouth.

-My dreams have taken on a different shape over the last couple days. They have become even more vivid than before...

-No more mysterious men lurking about? I said with a laugh.

She brushed off my attempt at humour with a scoff and pilfered a cigarette. I lacked the energy to stop her, even if I had tried. All I could do was listen to the unfolding narrative in a half conscious state, which seemed appropriate.

-Just to be clear, the man no longer has a face, but rather just a blank space where his features should be...

-Is the woman still there?

Marion got up and walked to the window and lit her cigarette with the candle before she blew it out. Her face was pale in growing light, which I realized was not that unusual for her, but this time it was somehow different.

-Yes, the woman is still there, only this time she has become two people. She split in two.

-Why does this scare you so much? I mean, they're just dreams after all, right?

She shook her head.

-You don't understand. Why did I bother calling you? I should have stayed away from Midtown for good.

I didn't know what to say. My body and mind couldn't form the words.

-What do you see in your dreams? she asked suddenly.

-Snowfalls. Empty skies at night. Rivers...

-And what do you make of them? Are they fluff, or do they disturb you and shake you to the core?

-I...don't know...Why?

-I ask because mine are often more real to me than these walls and what lives outside. That's where I live now, and it's terrifying. What do you find terrifying?

-Mantra Hand.

She looked at me as if to say "you're fucking crazy" without actually saying it.

-Do you think I look like him, Marion? I asked in a slur.

-Like who, Mantra Hand?

-Yeah...like him.

-No one really knows what he looks like do they? I mean, wasn't he a kind of recluse or something? I shouldn't have given you those pills.

I chuckled to myself. Marion stared out the window as the record player skipped in the background.

She was right, she shouldn't have given me the pills. I awoke from the haze to diminishing light and the skipping record. Marion had left, and the parts of Mantra's diaries I had been carrying in the book were scattered about the room. I called out to her. Nothing. Looking out the kitchen window, I could see that night was closing in. Picking up the book and the pages I decided to leave. Gently closing the door to her apartment, I slithered down the hall barely able to keep myself erect.

Even the fresh air that carried the scent of the coming fall did nothing to wake my senses.

Pausing on Salamander Road, I lit my final cigarette; Marion had taken the rest. As I walked I recalled a conversation we had had years before in the Outskirts...I was looking out the window at the Midtown skyline...

-When I'm gone, don't forget me.

-You're leaving? she asked curiously

-Yeah. I'm thinking about heading to Turkey. Anywhere really. I need to get away for a while and see what's out there.

-Why now?

-Boredom? Apathy? I'm not sure, exactly, but I need to go.

-How will I find you?

-Don't come looking for me.

She seemed saddened by my comment. I hate to think that contributed to something breaking inside her. I turned toward the window and watched the autumn leaves fall to the ground. I felt a glow inside me and suddenly everything became soft and settled. She stared at me as though she were expecting more, perhaps even an apology of some kind, but instead I spoke obscurely.

-Look for me between the notes of your favourite song, on the pages of a rare novel, or if you're daring, in the breadth of space between the Bosphorus and some majestic river.

-You really have a flair for the dramatic, don't you? she said with a hint of annoyance.

-No more than the next man, whoever he may be.

-The next man is someone we never see. It's like when people say they. Who are they, exactly? I think you're deliberately acting this way just to have me think you're more mysterious than you are.

I knotted my eyebrows.

-You don't think there is much to me, then?

-No more than the next man.

A sarcastic grin crossed her face.

I don't remember much after that point. Memory doesn't always yield gold; more often than not we're left with the tired remnants of situations best left unremembered. For a moment I wondered if her initial disappearance had anything to do with me. I felt a stream of warm tears fall down my face...The night had taken her again and I didn't know where to go. The streets were unbearably quiet. A deep silence never does wonders to someone preoccupied with unpleasant thoughts and I needed a cigarette badly. Looking at the pavement, I searched for something to smoke. Hands sifting through ash bins, eyes open wide, frantic for nicotine. Nothing. I stopped. "What was I doing?" I asked myself. My tears turned to laughter. In the distance, the dull lights of the Dragon Court beckoned me. An internal compass was pointing me toward my destination even if I hadn't realized it at the time. The closer I got, the colder I felt. It clung to my bones. Mantra Hand was right: Midtown was a strange city that seemed to swallow the unsuspecting at any turn. In that moment I didn't care.

I didn't look back.

....

A few mescaline dealers hovered around the Pavilion Arcade, along with the usual rag-tag bunch of smuggled in prostitutes who probably had only ever heard of Midtown in textbooks. They looked at me suspiciously as I slowly passed by. Brazenly, I asked one for a cigarette which she reluctantly pulled from her snakeskin purse. I lit it with relish and inhaled deeply.

-You must be a local, she croaked.

-Why do you say that? I asked with a smile.

-Everyone around here looks like they want to get out, including you.

-Stick around for a while and you'll want out too.

-What's that supposed to mean, exactly? she said with a hiss.

-Hang around here long enough and you'll find out.

I walked off, feeling somewhat more relaxed now that the nicotine was flowing through my system. At the far end of the Arcade I stopped. The door of the Arcana was before me once more, only this time there was no one to greet me. Stepping inside, the lighting and general ambiance felt different, warmer. A couple well-dressed men sat on the couch drinking, not even glancing in my direction as I walked in. I was confused. Taking a seat at the bar I waited for the masked women to appear. They were nowhere to be seen.

After a handful of minutes a youngish looking man came out of the back to serve me.

-What are you drinking tonight?

I had no energy to speak, so I simply pointed to a large scotch bottle and held up two fingers. Smiling, he prepared my drink, somehow knowing I wanted it neat. I stared at the amber liquid for a long time hoping it would reveal something to me, like an idiot. Then I felt someone sit down next to me.

-I didn't figure you for a scotch drinker. Maybe more of a rye or rum man? I'm glad I was wrong.

He motioned for a glass and moved his chair in a little closer. I looked at him carefully but I didn't know his face. He thanked the bartender for the scotch and took a hearty swig.

-Who might you be?

-Oh you know who I am, because I certainly know who you are.

It sounded so cliché, but at the same time I winced.

-Well you certainly can't be who I'm looking for.

-Who is that?

I laughed and finished my scotch, gesturing for another.

-One thing that's for certain is that you're not Mantra Hand. From what I've been reading he blew this pop stand a while back.

-I see. Well, I guess I won't waste your time then with idle chit-chat. I mean, really what does it matter if Mantra Hand is alive or dead?

-Funny you should say that...I was saying the same thing to myself earlier today. But seriously, who the fuck are you?

-I'm William Pawel, and I've been looking for you.

-Don't fuck with me, buddy...I'm not in the mood.

-You don't even want to know why I've been looking for you? This is a truly serendipitous event. I want to impart something to you. Don't tell me that you haven't been hoping to find me, because I'm sure you have lots of questions.

I downed my scotch in one go, not wanting to look him in the face. He offered me a smoke, which I gladly accepted without turning toward him. I rubbed my eyes, still feeling the heaviness of the Ativans in my head.

-Do you know this place well? I asked casually.

-By this place are you just referring to the Arcana, or to Midtown as a whole?

-The Arcana....Where are all the women?

-The first thing I can tell you is that your desires follow you wherever you go in this city. As time progresses those desires will actualize themselves.

-Kind of like the law of attraction? I scoffed.

-More like the phenomenon known as the Muted Horn.

-Why doesn't it surprise me that I'm the only one who knows nothing about it?

-Because you don't seem to care. You remind me a lot of him, you know?

-You mean Mantra Hand? I'm honoured...or at least I

think I am, depending on where you're going with this.

He showed a weak smile, sipping his scotch coolly before continuing.

-For one, Mantra Hand was a pessimist at heart. He was the product of a strict religious upbringing, but that changed as he developed his warped worldview. In fact, one could say it changed drastically when he met Miss Red.

-Miss Red? Is that the R. he speaks of in the letters?

-Undoubtedly. You see, we both were her lovers and she demonstrated an even deeper intelligence and fascination with death than he did. It's not hard to see why he would be attracted to her, even though I'm sure he played the passive role.

-Hard to imagine Mantra Hand being passive.

-Is it? Do you think that because he wrote brilliantly but arrogantly, and that he saw himself as a genius? You only know his words, you don't know the man.

-That may be true, but his archive seems to suggest something deeper and more revealing...the guy was fucking going crazy.

Pawel didn't say anything. I was still having a hard time believing that it was him in the first place, and that fate or what have you brought him to me so easily. Still, what he was saying resonated with a feeling inside me that I couldn't explain, so I went along.

-Let's get out into the air.

-We're leaving?

-Don't worry about your drinks, they're taken care of.

As we walked toward the door, I looked around hoping to catch a glimpse of something familiar...Nothing. The Arcana on that night was just another lounge in the Pavilion Arcade. Pawel looked at me with a grin, reading my expression of disorientation and more than a little disbelief. He opened the door for me and the smell of rain greeted us with open arms. I thought of Sandra and Marion, but I could only picture them in the colourful masks I had seen the night before, which made little or no sense.

-Can I ask where we're going?

-Someplace quiet and unassuming.

We walked for a long time, past familiar landmarks that

suddenly seemed out of place or distorted, barren streets and shuttered buildings, until we crossed the river at the High Gate bridge and made our way into the Waterfront Market. Entering one of the bars, he took me to an antechamber at the back, full of books and interesting miscellanea. I assumed it all belonged to him.

-I'm under the impression you know a lot of these works on my walls. If I'm correct, you have some sort of idea as to at least one side of Mantra Hand, the side that saw the Void.

-I've read a number of your works in the past, and virtually all of them deal with the esoteric beginnings of this city, so I fail to see the connection...

-Of course you do. But as I'm sure you are aware, being such a devotee of Mantra's works, you can see there was a piercing nihilism growing with each subsequent work. I would guess that those diaries you possess are a kind of final statement of intent.

-Maybe... I haven't read them all yet.

Pawel turned toward the bookshelf and pondered for a

moment. My face began to sweat and I felt uncomfortable in my chair. I still clutched my copy of *The Black Roses*, where the remaining shards of the diary stuck out. He noticed my agitation and offered me a glass of water which I declined.

-So what was your intent with all this Mantra Hand business anyway? Did his manuscripts showing up across your desk excite you substantially? Was your life lacking so much meaning that you had to attach yourself to his?

I winced.

-At this point, I just want to find my friend...

-And who might that be?

-Her name is Marion...she's not well.

-You don't look so well yourself, you know? Have a drink...

He handed me a glass filled with a dark blue liquid that smelled vaguely like rose petals. I sipped it cautiously.

-What you need to do is forget about Mantra Hand. Whether he found meaning or not is really none of our business. The only matter of importance is what will become of this city one day, maybe even in your lifetime. Perhaps it has already begun.

-What would that be? Or are you going to continue playing the role of mysterious stranger and let me figure it out on my own?

He laughed.

-To be quite honest I think you already have, inadvertently of course, through Mantra's works.

He saw what Red saw...I saw it as well...or at least I think I have.

He fell silent and turned away from me. I sipped the blue liquid, finding it suddenly warm and calming. So much so that I began to fall asleep in the chair I was sitting in. Flashes of tepid images flitted around my head. I dropped the glass but heard no crash.

narrow corridors   shadows   a view of the ocean

people talking in low voices

white ceramic houses

a railway track off in the distance

a knife being sharpened by suntanned hands

Then black, only black.

When I shook myself from the inner vision, Pawel, or who I thought was Pawel, was gone. I walked back into the bar and it was completely desolate and lifeless, and the lights were off. I placed my head in my hands, wondering what the hell he had given me. My hands shook and my body felt cold and damp even though the rain had stopped. Fumbling for my cell phone I tried calling Sandra. A message came on saying the number was no longer in service. I looked at the phone in disbelief. Pulling up the collar on my coat, I stared at the glowing phosphorescence reflecting in the water, creating a sea of light beneath my feet. Stopping in front of a store window, my blurred reflection seemed foreign. It was as though my face were no longer mine but deeply reminiscent of someone else entirely. My feet continued to carry me forward but my surroundings seemed increasingly unfamiliar. I don't remember where I slept that night, but I felt warm and somewhat comfortable in the darkness I inhabited. Using the glow of a lighter I continued to read...

(Shuttered Room)

This is a farewell as much as it is a letter to let you know I'm doing well where I am now, far from the crowds and mysteries of Midtown. The room is sparse, but I find it next to impossible to rid myself of books, music, and the occasional prostitute. Let's suffice to say that I'm comfortable and planning my next move, despite my current quotidian routine. What is the next move, you might ask? I'm not entirely certain of my motives beyond an overwhelming philosophical motive that continues to grow in bizarre ways each day, between hours of extreme despair and creative highs. I've once again found my calling, which can only continue to find its way into actuality within the flesh of humans. My artistic vision, as one might call it, is quickly becoming a twofold endeavour: in one respect with the pen, and the other with the sword...

....

...She sits by herself looking at the night sky, perhaps pondering why she is here in much the same way I've done a million times, no closer to the answer. The city sleeps in a vacuum-like silence. I fade into the lobby but continue to watch her through the slightly smoked glass. She looks so much like her...or *both of them*, wrapped together in a sweet bodily embrace. Her hair is a lunar yellow...papers drift down the empty streets, a few signs flash. Home so far behind me now. Home is nowhere. The light dims inside, setting the mood...a look of contentment etched on her face. Good, very good. Her eyes are of someone who has been waiting for rain here in the desert for many years. Maybe that truly was an angel dropping from the sky, landing in the shaded path in front of me...I can't believe my luck.

Does she see me glaring at her through the glass? No, no, her head is tilted toward the moon, full and pulling the sea again. I sit down again a few tables away from her, watching every subtle movement.

-Care for a drink, sir?

The lips move slowly and I barely hear the question.

-Double...double scotch, yes scotch please...yes.

-Very good, then.

Are we the only ones here now? I look around and see

only her. Calling back the waiter, whose face seems oddly pale and morose, I send a drink to her table. The waiter subtly points to me, and she looks at me with a smile and hoists the drink in the air as if to say cheers or thank you. Bait taken. I see the diamond glint in her eye, even from this distance. She is intrigued. The bar is now the stage upon which I step to work a foreign magic.

-Sorry for intruding on your evening, but you looked in need of some company. May I join you?

-Certainly, be my guest. What's your name?

-Mantra. Yours?

-Caissa.

-Pleased to make your acquaintance.

She is cautious. I can tell by the uneasiness with which she sips her drink and the gaze she gives me as I sip mine. Her neck is milk white and she smells of cinnamon. A copy of Foucault's *Death and the Labyrinth* lays on the chair beside her, which takes me a little by surprise, as I didn't see her carrying anything as I followed her here.

-Is Mantra your real name, or are you just in the habit of taking on aliases?

-It's my name. I legally changed it years ago when I felt a need for something new.

-Something new? Your old life didn't suit you then?

-You could say that.

-Where are you from? You're not a local...you have the look of someone who is lost, or looking for something.

-Maybe I was looking for you.

She blushes slightly, but she does her best to hide it. We finish our drinks and I order two more.

-Seriously though, where do you hail from?

-Midtown.

A look of surprise comes over her face, as though I spoke the wrong words.

-I've never met anyone from there...I've only heard the stories, as though it was a fabled place only found by people with a keen sense of direction.

-Like Melania or Adelma.

-I've never heard of those places. Do you visit them often?

-Friends and lovers have described them to me in detail. I've almost come to believe that they don't exist, like Shambhala or the Hidden Valleys of Shaolin. Images in a dream that quickly fades.

-So what about me? Am I a dream then? she says almost sarcastically.

I look at her closely, my vision blurred by the scotch.

-You are more real than anything else at the moment.

The air seems thicker and warmer. Too much scotch? I ask her if she wants to move the conversation outside, to which she agrees.

We ignore the new drinks on our table and I clear up the bill, even though it appears the waiter has vanished. The cool night air hits my lungs and I run my fingers through my hair and laugh out loud, my voice echoing down the empty street.

-The world is really just that funny isn't it?

I turn awkwardly toward her, forgetting that she's there.

-Yes...a very amusing world. One has to laugh in the face of the void or a little bit of the crazy will set in, unless it already has.

She hesitantly smiles at my remarks and I pause for a moment to light a fresh cigarette.

-Would you mind walking me back to my hotel, if it's not too much trouble? My fiancé was going back up the coast for a few days and I have no escort. I wouldn't ask normally, but it's getting late...

-No problem, angel. I should be getting to bed myself. You know, I never did ask you what your name meant. I've never heard it before, it's so unique.

She holds her book close to her chest, perhaps thinking that words will somehow protect her, for I can see that my presence is now only a matter of convenience. The moon is full tonight and its silken rays light our path through an otherwise barren city. We walk for a long time before she says anything.

-They say Caissa was the invention of a poet, but she was the goddess of chess players. My father was born in Europe and played at a competitive level. He suggested the name to my mother when I was born...

-Is that so? An old friend...a very old friend who I have not seen in a long time used to play chess quite avidly.

145

You remind me of her.

She can probably see the devil in my eyes by this point, but she doesn't back away, though she still keeps her distance. Her engagement ring looks cheap and dull, and she takes notice of my eyes wandering over her hand.

-We got engaged a few days ago. I never thought he would ask me. I'm not even sure why I'm telling you this, we're really just strangers.

-A stranger is just a friend you haven't met.

-Well, here's my hotel. Thanks for escorting me, and for the drinks.

-How about a nightcap?

-I think the hotel bar is closed by now...

-That's fine dear Caissa, perhaps we'll run into each other again soon.

She smiles at me weakly and walks through the door and out of sight. I toss my cigarette into the gutter, laughing at the moon. We'll meet again, and again and again before I leave this place. Heaven has finally smiled upon me, hasn't it?

As I walk through the valley of the shadow of death, I shall fear no evil...

....

...I opened my eyes and the first thing I could discern, other than the clamour around me, were the pages of the diary and The Black Roses which were burned around the edges. My body ached, but my mind felt strangely clear, almost buoyant. The encounters of the night before seemed almost unreal and I made my way by foot back toward the Outskirts and the Marble Corridor. As I walked, the city appeared as different as ever: the colours of familiar streets, vendors, even the commuters looked as though they had been dipped in sunshine, blissfully unaware that the sky was darkening above them.

My phone was nearly dead, but two messages had been left at some point during the night. Listening to both, I could make out faint voices that could have been Marion or Sandra, but mostly static and noise drifted into my ear. I threw the phone into a garbage can and kept walking. A little known path out of the city around the Corridor is where I headed as the hum of activity faded behind me. Once on the other side I sat down and breathed heavily, searching frantically for a death stick. None. All I had left was the book and diary entries, so I leaned against a light-post and read, my weary eyes scanning what was left of Mantra Hand...

(Visions)

I've been unable to move forward much, for I've not found the energy to do so in this endless space. Over the last day (days?) a rapid uneasiness has fallen upon me. Who? The Horn has been quiet as of late in this denseness. What? I do not know, this has all become a mystery to me. When? Long ago when I crossed the Threshold. Where? That I can't seem to remember with any kind of clarity. Why? In order to find her. The seeds were planted long ago before I ever met R. Perhaps my whole intent was to become one with them in flesh. What a stupid thought. R. got away from me too quickly for me to realize that perhaps my actions were in vain. No, no, my actions have begun to blossom, even though I have trapped myself here. As I said from the beginning, I will be liberated. I must be quiet now as I wait, for the sounds of the Horn may flood my ears at any minute. Nothing would sound sweeter at this point. Nothing.

Fitting. The almighty Mantra Hand destroyed by feminine force. The kinship I thought I felt melted away. We're not the same at all, I thought, smirking...Not the same in the least. Turning over the last page, however, I felt his cold hand one more time for good measure...

(Victim)

So the rest of the story goes as follows: 1. A true departure: 35.173808, -4.965820 2. A thorough examination of, and study of, the area in question. 3. Finding a suitable place for seduction. 4. IX°, possibly XI° 5. A drugging of some sort. Wine or opium. Preferably opium 6. Systematic carving and preservation of flesh for future. 7. Spend a week writing or travelling before continuing onto the next step. 8. Photograph results of step 6, make copies for delivery to random addresses. 9. Begin manuscript dealing with events or non-events and decide where to send. 10. Move. Staying in one place too long is not recommended, anywhere will do. 11. Once established in a new location, repeat steps 2 through 6. Create a pattern. 12. After the pattern has been thoroughly established, destroy the pattern entirely. 13*.?